DADDY'S LITTLE ANGEL

MIA CLARK

ISBN: 1987650395
ISBN-13: 978-1987650396

Book design by Cherrylily
Cover design by Cherrylily
Cover Image © Depositphotos | majdansky

Cherrylily.com

To Erica

Thank you again for helping me come up with the ideas in this story! You were a huge help and I will always appreciate you.

Love you!

~Mia

CONTENTS

ACKNOWLEDGMENTS

Thanks so much for taking a chance on my book!

I say that in every one of my paperback books, haha. I mean it, though! Every time you grab a new book you're always kind of taking a chance and hoping it'll be everything you could ever hope for, right?

Well, this one's definitely for you and here's what you can expect!

I love forbidden romance, but I like it with a more playful and fun side to it. I like getting into the romantic comedy aspects of relationships because I think it's important to have fun in life and I want my characters to do the same.

And, you know, they might wind up in some awkward situations along the way, but I think those are the best kinds, haha. My characters are never boring, that's for sure.

As far as the "Daddy" aspect to this book, I really like the more playful side of BDSM, and I thought it'd be fun to include that in some of my books. If you know what DD/lg is, then that's kind of what we're about to get into here. I don't go crazy and my characters don't even really talk about this, but...

Basically sometimes Fiona's a brat and sometimes Grey spanks her for it, but they both enjoy it and it's more fun than anything. Also since she likes it, he might have to come up with some new and creative ways to punish her but she might enjoy those, too...

Oh no!

A lot of this book deals with their age difference and the different issues that can arise because of that. Also, you know, she calls him Daddy, so that doesn't help. It started as a joke, and then they both liked it so they went with it.

Fiona is his sister's best friend, but she's got more than a few Daddy Issues of her own (and that's another book entirely, haha), so I think her and Grey are good for each other. They go together really well.

So... this is that kind of story. It's fun, with some sexy romance, a little bit of kink, some awkward situations, and two characters who can't get enough of each other in all ways possible. Their love is really fun.

Enjoy, and happy reading!

FOREWORD

Make sure you don't miss any of my new releases by
signing up for my VIP readers list!
Cherrylily.com/Mia
You can also find me on Facebook for more sneak peeks
and updates here:
Facebook.com/MiaClarkWrites

You can find all of my books on Amazon, including my
bestselling Stepbrother With Benefits series!
All of Mia Clark's Books

INTRODUCTION

Do you know how fucking hard it is to try and stop when you're ball's deep inside of the perfect little pussy of the more than perfect eighteen year old girl who's laying on your bed, legs spread wide for you and you alone? How the fuck am I supposed to handle a situation like this?

Probably by stopping. Except, you know, why stop, Grey? Just pound away, give her what she's been begging for this entire time. You teased her up to it, right? Well yeah, I did, and that was the plan, except then my little sister called.

What's that have to do with anything, you ask? Thanks. Thanks for fucking asking. Why do you have to ruin this for me? I'm already angry enough at myself for getting caught up in the moment with Fiona, so I could definitely use a reminder about how depraved I am.

The issue, the entire fucking problem, is that my little sister Emily called right in the middle of me and her best friend having fun. Oh, and Emily doesn't know that I'm fucking her best friend, so that's another issue right there. Plus they're on the phone together right now.

Yeah... think about that one for a second...

I slide out of Fiona's perfect fucking pussy until just the head of my cock is lodged between her smooth lips. Her eyes roll into the back of her head as I grind my way into her again. My balls lightly smack against her ass and I feel her clenching hard against my shaft.

Yeah, that's it. That's my good girl, Fiona. Take Daddy's cock. You can do it. Take it all, feel it, and give me your orgasm. That's what I want. That's what I...

The "Daddy" thing is a long story. It's probably even worse than you think. I know this is fucked up. I know I'm probably fucked up. Is that going to stop me? Have you even been paying attention?

Like I said before, I'm ball's deep inside of Fiona's perfect little pussy while she clamps down on me like she's going to die if I don't give her an orgasm soon. And she's talking on the phone with my sister at the same time.

"Mmmmm," she says, trying not to moan too loudly. "He's... Daddy's... *right there*... here! I meant he's right here! It's so much, though. *So full*. His hands, I mean! Um..."

Thanks, Fiona. Emily's not going to suspect a thing.

Yeah... we're screwed.

FIONA

How did I wind up on Daddy's bed, my legs spread wide for him, his *"almost too big, but, oh, I need it so bad"* cock inside me? That's a really great question! I don't even know where to start, so can we skip that part for now?

The thing is that ever since he let me move in with him, and ever since my best friend Emily, who just so happens to be Daddy's sister, went away to college, well...

Daddy gets really stressed sometimes from work. Also, I try so hard to be a good girl, but sometimes I end up teasing him a lot? It's not my fault, I swear! Um, no, it is my fault, and I'm so so sorry, Daddy, but I can make it better? If you need to punish me, I understand. I'll try not to do it again.

And if you need to unwind after work and let go of some of your stress, why don't you let go of it inside me?

Please, Daddy...

I want your cum so bad... I want to feel it deep in my tight

3

pussy and I want you to know how much I want it and how much it means to me...

So that's how that happened. That's how that kind of thing always happens, right? I don't know. I've only ever done this with Daddy, so I couldn't tell you, but I'm going to assume that this is how it happens for everyone. I sure hope so, at least. It's basically amazing.

Anyways, then Emily calls, and I sort of have to answer her because she keeps calling. I try to ignore it at first, and Daddy does, too. Except Emily calls again. And once more. Another time.

Daddy winces as the phone keeps ringing, and I don't want Daddy to be worried or stressed out. That's why we're doing this, so he can relax and release and give me his cum. He slows down from pounding away at my puffy little pussy--which is puffy all because of him, by the way. Thank you, Daddy!--and glances at my phone sitting on his bedside table.

"It probably won't take long," I tell him. "I can talk to her quick and tell her I'll call her back?"

This makes plenty of sense right now, because we've stopped for a second to talk about it, but I'm not going to lie, it's, um... sort of hard to put two and two together when I have Daddy's cock inside me. I'm not really thinking clearly at the moment. My mind is about to cum to a lot of cumclusions and I probably shouldn't try to cum up with ideas that don't involve what we've cum here to do.

Daddy doesn't say anything, just grunts and nods at me. It's sexier than I should probably admit, especially considering I have my phone in my hand and I'm about to answer a call from his sister. And my best friend. And...

"Hi!" I say, louder than I mean to. And then I let out a sharp squeak as Daddy thrusts his cock deep inside me. My eyes roll into the back of my head and I completely forget what I was just doing. Phone huh what?

"Fifi!" Emily says, giddy. And then a pause. "Are you alright? What's going on?"

"Oh, you know," I say. "The usual. Stuff. Things. Stuff and things."

I accidentally say the last part so it sounds exactly like "stuffing things" which is eerily accurate, but...

Act casual, Fiona! Try to pretend that Daddy's cock isn't deep inside you at this very moment. How do I even do that? He's not being as rough or as hard as before, but in a lot of ways that's even worse. I can feel every throbbing inch of him as he slides deep inside my overworked pussy. Daddy teased me relentlessly today, which is part of why I teased him back, and even when we ended up in his bed together he kept teasing and teasing. I need to cum around his cock just as much as I need him to cum inside me.

And I also sort of need to talk to Emily since I'm on the phone with her right now, so...

"Is something going on?" Emily asks, worry painted in her voice. "Where's Grey? He didn't leave you home alone, did he? I know you hate that."

"He's... Daddy's... *right there...*" I say, right as he hits the spot deep inside me that I love so much. What am I...? Oh,

5

right. "Here! I meant he's right here! It's so much, though. *So full*. His hands, I mean! Um..."

His hands are kind of full, so I don't think that's a lie? He's gripping my hips tight, pinning my waist to the bed as he grinds his cock into me. As soon as I say what I just said, he grins at me and keeps doing everything exactly the way he was. He lifts his hips up so that the base of his shaft teases against my clit, and he leans forward so he can keep up the momentum. I'm skewered on Daddy's cock, every single nerve in the center of my body sending out a rush of sensation to everywhere else in my body.

"I'm... I'm cumming..." I whimper as my world goes dark from ecstasy.

I can't see anymore, I don't even know what's going on. My body betrays me and I squeeze hard around Daddy's cock, clamping and clutching against him. Sparks burst forth behind my eyelids, a flash of light beneath my clenched shut eyes. A second later I feel Daddy giving me even more of what I needed. I really need a lot right now, too.

Yes, please, thank you, Daddy. I'll be your good girl forever. I just want you to feel good and I feel so good right now, also. I love your cum so much and I want it inside me all the time and...

I forget how long that goes on. I was talking to someone, right? Listless, I hold the phone in my hand, trying to remember what I was...

Oh shoot!

Emily.

"...Fiona?" she asks, clearly concerned. "Is--"

I cut her off, my mental clarity returning shortly after my ecstasy induced insanity. I... I plead the fifth! Can I do that? I don't know but I'm doing it.

"I'm coming to give Daddy the phone so you can talk to him!" I say, fast. It's the only thing that comes to my mind.

"You mean you're *going* to give it to him?" my best friend asks.

"Yup, um, sorry," I say, mumbling. "I meant I'm *going* to give it to him and he's *coming* to get it. He's just finishing up what he was doing, and... oh, look, he's done! Good job, Daddy!"

I mouth the words, "Thank you for *cumming* with me," and then I hand him the phone.

"Oh, uh, hey, Emily..." Grey says, slow.

I like how tired Daddy gets sometimes after he cums. Just a little sleepy, you know? He's always handsome, but when he's just a little bit tired I think he's extra handsome, especially because then we get to cuddle a lot. I love when Daddy lays on his side and he pulls me up close to him and we spoon together while the both of us are still naked and I can feel his cum sliding out of me.

I also like when Daddy doesn't get tired after and he wants to do it again. Both are fun. This is one of his sleepy times, though.

He gently pats my pussy to show me what a good girl I've been, and then he slowly pulls his cock out of me. Careful, he slides up the bed and lays down next to me. I put my arm over his chest and cuddle up close to him, watching Daddy talk to Emily.

I wish we could tell her. I don't want her to be mad at

me. I think she'd understand, but I don't really know. Maybe she'd understand but she'd still be mad?

The thing is, Daddy is all Emily has. He's not her real father, he's her older brother, but their parents had an unfortunate accident and he kind of ended up having to take over as the head of the household. There's a lot more to it and Daddy explains it better than I can.

He's not my actual father, either. I don't even know who my real dad is. I've never known. Emily and I became friends in high school, and then I started coming over to her house after school a lot more, and one day I was teasing Grey so I asked Emily if I could call him Daddy, too, and...

I liked it? A lot? Mhm...

I still like it. I know Grey's not my real father and I don't want him to be. I want him to be my Daddy in a different way, though. It doesn't have to make sense to anyone else, it just has to make sense to me and him.

And hopefully Emily...

3
GREY

Why am I talking on the phone with Emily again? Seriously, that was Fiona's job. You had one job, Fiona! My job was to fill Fiona the fuck up, which I'd been trying to do for a few minutes until my sister kept calling and interrupting us, and...

I mean, Fiona's full now, her tight pussy completely stuffed with my cum, so... good job to me?

I'm fucked up, aren't I? Look, there's more to my relationship with Fiona than just sex, but sometimes you need to get the sex parts out of the way so you can get to the rest. Uh, fuck, I meant... it's not like it's a chore. Having sex with Fiona is literal heaven, except then every time we do it I feel like I'm going to Hell after.

Not a deep and resounding feeling of doom or anything. No, just a few nagging thoughts. It's like, yeah, Grey, why are you fucking the shit out of your sister's best friend? She's eighteen and you're thirty, so that's kind of a big age gap. And she calls you Daddy for fuck's sake! What the hell, man?

It's not just sex, though. Fiona and I go to yoga together, and she helps me out at home. We cuddle and watch movies. We talk a lot. She hasn't really had the best home life growing up, so I want to make sure she's happy and safe. I also want her to make something of herself.

She doesn't *have* to. I'm not pressuring her into shit here. That's what she wants to do, so I want to help her do it. I'm not here to brag, but if I'm being honest I could support myself, Fiona, and even give Emily whatever money she needs, and we'd all be fine for the rest of our lives. My parents left me everything, which included the house and their business, and I've done my best to grow it into something amazing. I really think they'd be proud of me.

Except maybe not considering this whole fucking the shit out of Emily's best friend thing. I don't know if they'd be proud of that one. Hey, nobody's perfect, alright?

Anyways, after filling Fiona the fuck up with my cum and making sure she got hers, I'm somehow on the phone with my sister.

Fiona's cuddling with me, too. Naked. We're both naked. I feel like I should put some clothes on, but Fiona's a literal cuddlebug after sex and I kind of love it, so not only can I not get up and get dressed right now, but I don't want to.

"So, uh, how's college?" I ask. Keep it safe. Stick to the basics, Grey.

"What are you doing to Fiona?" Emily asks, glaring at me through the phone.

I don't know how I know she's glaring at me, but she's my sister. Trust me when I say she's glaring at me. I know all about these things.

"To what are you referring?" I ask. Belatedly, I realize, uh... who the fuck even says something like that?

"She sounded upset," Emily says, this time narrowing her eyes at me. "I know work is stressful sometimes and you get in a grumpy mood, but don't take it out on Fiona, Grey! Don't be mean to her!"

When my sister calls me Grey instead of Daddy, you know she's serious. Also, what the fuck? I wasn't even being mean to Fiona. I was being so fucking nice, pun intended. I mean, I may have spanked her here and there, but sometimes she's a naughty girl and, let's be honest, she enjoys it.

I enjoy doing it too, but that's beside the point.

"Look," I say, being straight with her. "I wasn't being mean to Fiona. She was just, uh..."

Think, Grey. What was she doing besides moaning and clenching against your cock before cumming hard?

"Uh huh?" Emily asks, completely doubting everything I say. We're supposed to be family, Emily. I can't even believe this. You doubt your own brother? Wow.

"She was practicing her splits," I say. There we go! It's not entirely a lie, right? Her legs were spread pretty far, so... "Yeah, I was in the kitchen putting groceries away and Fiona was practicing her splits. She's getting good at it. Some real intense shit right there, and--"

11

"Daddy!" Emily says. "Language!"

Holy shit, my sister, the proper fucking language police over here. If she knew some of the things her best friend's said when my cock's deep inside her, or about to be inside her, or when she wants it inside her, I really don't think she'd start with me on this one. Or she still would. Fiona and I should probably tell Emily what's up sooner rather than later, it's just, uh...

How do I even begin to explain this to my little sister? I never meant for this to happen, it just sort of did, and I'm real fucking glad it did, but...

"Anyways, what's up, twerp?" I ask. Yeah, keeping it cool over here. "You good? College going well? When are you coming back home to visit?"

"Actually!" Emily says, practically squealing the word. "You know Valentine's Day is soon, right? Do you have a date?"

"What, me, uh?" I say, and then I follow up with my great standby question of, "To what are you referring?"

Seriously, what the fuck am I doing here?

"I would say it'd be fun if you and Fiona went out for a nice dinner, but I'm stealing her away!" Emily says, giggling. "That's what I called about. There's a frat here that's hosting a Valentine's Day single's party."

"A frat?" I ask, immediately feeling an emotion I don't know how to explain.

Let's try, though. Here's the explanation. My sister wants to go to a frat party. For Valentine's Day. It's for people who are single. Every dude there is going to be single. With my sister. And on top of that she wants Fiona to go?

Are you fucking with me? Why is this a thing that's happening? What did I do to deserve this?

This is my punishment for fucking my little sister's best friend behind her back, isn't it?

Holy fucking shit...

"It's a very established and dignified fraternity house," Emily adds, gushing about this party she's apparently going to without my permission. Seriously, doesn't she have to ask me if she can go to shit like this? I think she does.. "It's the Sigma Epsilon Chi frat. I know Fiona doesn't go to college here, but no one will know. I figured if you were going to be in the area for work, she could come with you and then Fiona and I could go together? That would actually be really great, too, because, so... I'm not saying we're going to drink, so don't go all parental mode on me here, but if something happens it would be really great to have someone we trust that we can call to come help us out, you know?"

Now she wants my help? Since I'm her legal guardian, can't I ground her or something? Yeah, she's in college, but so what? That's helping, right? There's your help, Emily. No. No fucking way. You're grounded. Go study or something. Fuck Valentine's Day!

No. Shit. Don't... don't fuck on Valentine's Day. Don't fuck at all!

Yes, I'm a huge fucking hypocrite. Sorry? I'm older and more mature or something so it's fine. It's different. Maybe.

"Wait, did you say Sigma Epsilon Chi?" I ask, putting a few things together. Emily's all crickets on the other end of the phone. "Uh... S.E.X., Emily? Really? What kind of frat is this?"

"It's... it's just a joke, Daddy," Emily says, going on the defensive. "You know how guys are. It's not serious. The college makes them put S.E.C. on their official notices and on the frat house door, but they always spell it with an X for the parties and stuff. It's not, um..."

"So," I say, interrupting her. "Let me guess. This is something like... let me give this a shot. The Valentine's Day Single's Sigma Epsilon Chi Party? Seriously, Emily? The Valentine's Day Single's S.E.X. Party?"

"Wow, you got it right on the first try," my little sister says, somehow impressed. "Huh!"

I know how the fuck college works, Emily. I've seen some shit you wouldn't even believe.

"I'm not letting my little sister go to a sex party," I tell her. "No fucking way."

"Daddy!" she whines. "It's not a sex party! It's just a joke. I can send you the email about it. The one for parents. It's actually for a great cause."

Yeah, sure. What the fuck bullshit is that? A Valentine's Day single's sex party for the environment! To feed the homeless! For literacy or something?

The email they send out to parents is probably one-hundred percent bullshit, too. I know how this works, little sister of mine.

And... no. No fucking way am I buying that. I don't

14

believe it. And I tell my sister that. Not in as many words. Why use a lot when you can use one?

"No."

"Hmph!" she harrumphs at me. Probably would cross her arms over her chest and glare except she can't since she's holding her phone. Maybe she does it one handed. "Let me talk to Fiona again. Ugh! You're so--"

I don't really fucking care what I'm "so--" right now. I'm so fucking over Emily's shit, that's what I'm "so--."

Also, there's no fucking way I'm letting Fiona go to some college frat party. Because I'm a greedy asshole, that's why. Yes, at one point I thought she should probably go date some guys her own age, and... technically speaking if it wasn't Fiona we're talking about I might still think that's true. I don't think I'm good for her, even if it feels so fucking good to be with her.

I don't want my sister to be single forever, either. I want some nieces and nephews some day. I'm not really looking forward to doing that whole "What are your intentions with my little sister?" thing that our dad would have had to do. Or I *am* looking forward to it, but Emily won't. This guy better be a fucking saint if he wants to date my sister. I know what kids your age think about, buddy. Don't even fucking think about it with my sister, though! She's...

I don't know. Emily's not an idiot or anything. I doubt she'd fall for some shitty dude's shitty pickup lines. She's probably fine.

That doesn't mean I want Fiona going to some frat sex party, though.

I'm all for Emily's first suggestion: Fiona and I going

out for a nice Valentine's Day dinner. Why don't we do that one? Sounds real fucking good to me, so...

"Yup," Fiona says, nodding into the phone. "Uh huh. Yes. I'll... I'll try? Yup!"

None of this sounds good. I don't like it.

FIONA

I'm torn in more ways than one and I don't know what to do or say about it. I want to make Daddy happy, but Emily's my best friend and I want her to be happy, too.

And... I get to be happy, right?

I am! I really am happy, and it's not like I'm mad or upset or sad or anything. I love being with Daddy, even if we're keeping it a secret for now. Grey is literally the most important man in my life, and he's been that way for a long time.

He's been the only important man I've ever had in my life and I love him so much and I like calling him Daddy and watching him smile when I'm a good girl, or if I'm a little naughty he gets this really sexy glint in his eyes. Those are the times I know I'm about to be punished, and I probably deserve it, but also Daddy is so very nice to me and he wouldn't ever hurt me.

But then there's Emily, who's been my best friend for slightly longer. I knew her before I knew her brother if we're being one-hundred percent honest. Most of the time we all hung out together when Emily and I went over to her house. We never went to my house, because, um... I don't really like talking about that one. It's still hard for me to deal with. Anyways, we've all spent so much time together, and I have other friends and stuff, but Emily's my best friend.

I totally get where Daddy is coming from. I'm not sure that I should be going to some frat house sex party. I wouldn't do anything bad though, Daddy! Promise! Emily said it's just a joke, too. It's not really a sex party, that's just their Greek letters. Which, um...

"Daddy?" I ask him while we cuddle and he runs his fingers through my hair. Emily's invitation is still on both of our minds, even if we hung up with her a few minutes ago. "How's the fraternity thing work? How does Sigma Epsilon Chi mean sex?"

Daddy pulls me close and kisses the top of my head. I nuzzle into his arms and rest my head on his chest, listening to the rhythmic beat of his heart.

"It's the Greek alphabet," he says. "Sort of. The letters look different than ours. None of them looks like an 'S' actually, so I guess it's not quite the same. The frat probably took some liberties there. sigma's more like a sideways 'M' and then epsilon is a stylized 'E.' Chi looks like an 'X' and it's pronounced similarly even though the letter has a completely different sounding name. If you put them all together, in Greek it would be pretty close to sounding like 'sex' if you said it out loud."

"Oh," I say. "Huh! It doesn't mean the same thing, right? In Greek, I mean?"

Daddy laughs a little and I smile into his chest. "No, probably not. I'm not actually sure how you say 'sex' in Greek. I just know a few things about fraternities and letters from when I was younger."

"Were you ever in one?" I ask him, curious.

I can't picture Daddy being the same as my mental image of a frat boy. I mean, I don't know a lot about them, but I've seen some movies. Those are probably exaggerated, though.

"I wanted to be when I was younger," he says, oddly truthful and with a hint of wistfulness in his voice. I didn't expect this answer. "I didn't exactly have the standard college experience since I had to take care of Emily," he adds. "Not that, uh... I didn't mean it like that, Fiona. I didn't mean it in a bad way."

"I know," I say, kissing his naked chest. "You love Emily. I know it was hard for you. I don't know all of it, but I've been around you two for long enough to know how it is."

We're still naked and I love cuddling with Daddy like this. It's different from having sex. Being naked and being together is really nice in its own way and I feel so warm and close to him when we're like this.

"Yeah..." he says, trailing off, lost in whatever thoughts are bustling through his mind at the moment.

"Do you think that frats are like in the movies?" I ask him.

"Probably not," he says, chuckling. "Do you know

what the point of a frat is? What they're supposed to be about?"

"Um, I know it's a brother thing, I think?"

"Right," he says, teasing some of my hair and curling it around his finger. "Fraternities and sororities are supposed to be a brotherhood or sisterhood, literally. They're intended to be for networking purposes between students that have similar goals, and a lot of them do charity work and help out in their local communities."

"So they're good?" I ask, because... I don't know... I've seen some movies, let me tell you.

"Maybe," Grey grunts, sounding annoyed with himself. "Technically it's possible. Did Emily put you up to this?"

He looks down at me, my cheek on his chest while he plays with my hair. I look up at him and I bat my eyelashes a little, because it's fun to see how Daddy looks at me when I do that. He hides a grin, and I know he's looking at my eyes right now and even if he's trying to be grumpy he loves me and he likes me a lot. Not because we just had sex, but because he's my Daddy.

"Nope!" I say, sticking my tongue out at him. "I'm just curious, that's all. I'm wondering about stuff."

"What kind of stuff are you wondering about?" he asks, his expression softening.

"Well, I really want to go to college, but I don't know how, and I don't want to ask you to pay for it. I wouldn't do that and even if you said you would, I wouldn't let you. I want to do it on my own and show you that I can, because I think that would make you really proud of me, which would make me happy. And, so, college is more than just studying, right? There's a lot going on. Like this party that Emily wants to go to, or I could join a sorority. I don't know if I'd want to do that. Do you think they'd like me?"

"What? Why wouldn't they like you?" he asks, completely appalled at the idea that somehow someone in the world wouldn't like me. This is probably one of the reasons I love Daddy so much.

"I mean... we're dating, right? You and I. And I call you Daddy, so... I really like it, and I like being your good girl, and even if you have to spank me sometimes or punish me like you did when we went to the grocery store the other day, um... I don't know. Are there other girls like me that I could talk to? I don't want people to think I'm weird, but maybe I'm weird."

"I love your weirdness," Daddy says, pulling me up and kissing my cheek. "I'm sure there's sororities who would have girls in them that... yeah, I don't know. Let's look into it if you really want to go to college."

"I do!" I say, excited. "I think it'd be really fun and I think I'd like to talk to other girls about... stuff... I don't know, um... can I talk to people about us? I know we haven't told Emily, so..."

"I, uh... yeah..." Daddy says, slow and full of thoughts. "I really want to. You're special to me, Fiona. I get it, too. We've talked about this before and I think you should go to college and I'll help you figure out how you can do it, but if I'm being completely honest, I'm worried."

"What are you worried about?" I ask him. I know the answer, but I want to hear Daddy tell me.

"You," he says. "Or more like us. I mean, look, I'm being selfish and I want you all to myself. I know it's probably wrong. You're Emily's best friend, and... yeah... I know that deep down you should probably explore life and have relationships with boys your own age. I wouldn't stop you if that's what you decided you needed to do, but that's what hurts. That's not what I want and I know this is wrong, so, uh..."

"Nope!" I say, pressing my nose to his and shaking my head so our noses brush together, side to side. "I don't want other boys. I don't want anyone else. I want you, so you're stuck with me!"

He smiles and sneaks in close, kissing me. I flutter my eyelashes at him, tickling both of ours together in a butterfly kiss mixed with a regular kiss. I love touching Daddy and kissing him and smiling at him. And...

I feel Daddy between my legs. His cock throbs slightly, not fully hard but more than hard enough that I could easily slip him inside me if I shifted a little. I don't, not yet. Maybe soon, but I just want to kiss him and be close to him right now.

"So you want to go to this Valentine's Day party, huh?" he asks, our lips still close together.

"Yes, and I promise to be the goodest girl in the history of good girls," I tell him.

"The goodest girl, eh?" he asks, smirking at him.

"Greatest girl doesn't really sound the same, but I want to be that, too," I add.

"Good," he says, pressing his lips to mine quick. "I guess... I mean, if anyone can make sure Emily stays out of trouble, it's probably you. And I want you to know that I do trust you, Fiona. This isn't about that."

"I know," I say, smiling at him and closing my eyes, contented. "Not everyone is like you, Daddy. I know that, too. Believe me, I do! Ugh."

He laughs softly. "Yeah, I guess you would, huh?"

"You'll be close by too, right?" I ask. "If we go up to visit Emily and you stay in a hotel like you do when we go there for your work, you'll be around in case something happens?"

His pupils flash, a quick dilation, and then he tries to hide his sudden burst of anxiety over something--*anything*--bad happening.

"Yeah," he says, his voice deceptively calm and gentle. "I'll be there. Maybe we'll stay in a different hotel this time. One closer to this frat house. I'll look into it."

"Yay!" I say, kissing his cheek. "I love you, Daddy."

"I love you too, brat," he says, grinning at me.

"Nope! I'm your good girl, not a brat."

"Yeah, well, any excuse I can use to spank your ass, I'll gladly take it, so you better be extra good..."

"What if you spank me as a reward?" I ask, coy, looking away from him. "I really like rewards like that, too..."

"We can talk about rewards," he says. "Soon. You want to call Emily back and tell her I agreed to let you go to the party, right? I can tell. You go do that and I'll get dressed and then let's clean up this place a little and figure every-thing out."

"I do want to call Emily..." I say, slow. "But can you wait until after to get dressed? I want to take a shower with you. I like when you wash my hair. Is that alright?"

"Of course it is," Daddy says, smiling sweetly at me. "Go on. I'll wait for you."

"Alright. I'll be quick," I say, giddy.

I roll away from him and off the bed to grab my phone from his bedside table. Before I can scurry away and head to my own bedroom upstairs to call Emily, Daddy reaches out and smacks my butt. I jump, surprised, and then I spin around and point a finger at him.

"Be good!" I say, laughing. "Down boy!"

"Oh, I'm a dog now?" he asks, pretending to snarl and growl at me.

"I mean, you do like doggystyle, so..."

"Yeah, keep it up, Fiona. You're done," Daddy says, his eyes glimmering with a sudden intense desire.

I can tell because I feel it, too. Heat and need pools in my stomach and between my legs, and I know that if I don't hurry away fast, we're going to end up in the exact position I just said and neither of is going to get anything done for at least another hour.

I like that, and I love when Daddy takes me like that, but... I'm a good girl right now! I just promised I would be the goodest girl, and I'm already doing a bad job of it. Good girls know that they can't tease their Daddy so much that he keeps her naked and in his bed all day and doesn't get any work done.

And even if Daddy is letting me live with him, I need to be responsible and try to make something of myself. I want to, even.

"Sorry for being a brat just now," I say, flashing him a silly pout. "I'll be good, alright? But... if we're both good can we do that later? I really want to but I know you have to do work and we need to clean and will you go to yoga with me this afternoon, too?"

"Yes," he says, smiling wide at me. "I'll get the shower ready for us. Hurry up, baby girl."

"Yes, sir!" I say, teasing him one last time and giving him a quick salute.

Just a little tease, I swear! I scamper out of Daddy's bedroom with my phone, naked, and hop up the stairs to my own new bedroom. Once I get to the top of the stairs, I dial Emily and then dash into my room and leap onto the bed.

5

FIONA

Emily pauses, her silence anxiety-inducing, and I start to worry that maybe I said something wrong, until finally she says, "So Daddy agreed to let us go to the party? I was kind of going to sneak over either way, but I really wanted you to go with me. What'd you do to convince him?"

Oh no. What did I do to convince him? Eek! What do I tell her? What do normal people say? I can't tell her that Daddy and I were laying naked in his bad after he came inside me, which actually happened when Emily and I were on the phone earlier, but let's not bother with those details. Or any details! No details!

And so we were cuddling naked, me and Daddy, and he was playing with my hair. I like when he twirls some of my hair around his finger and when he teases and massages my scalp. That's also why I like when Daddy washes my hair for me. I mean, yes, I can wash my own hair, but massaging my own scalp isn't the same as Daddy doing it. When Daddy does it I basically melt, and I like when Daddy makes me melt. Sometimes it's a hot sexy melt, or other times it's a sweet cuddly melt, and all melting is good as far as I'm concerned as long as it's with Daddy.

Also he smacked my butt and I teased him about taking me doggystyle on his bed. I don't know if any of those had to do with how I convinced Daddy to let me and Emily go to the Sigma Epsilon Chi Valentine's Day party, but those are all the things that come to mind as soon as she asks that question.

"Fiona?" Emily asks from the other end of the phone, worried. "Oh no, did something happen! Grey's not being a creep, is he?"

"What! No?" I say. I meant to kind of reverse the exclamation and the question part of that, but I can't fix it now. "Um, so, he... he said there's business he has to do. It's all very work-related. On the up and up."

That's what people say when they do work stuff, right? Don't worry, everything's on the up and up. I think that's how this works.

"It's on the up and up?" Emily asks, obviously confused. "What's that mean?"

"Oh, you know," I say, aiming for an absent-minded approach. I add a little "ha ha" to really make it work. "He's, um... it's a lot of stuff."

Stuff. Yup. Great job, Fiona! You're really selling this one.

"Fifi, you're being weird," Emily says.

28

"I'm not a dog, Emily. Ugh! That nickname is dumb. No one else even calls me that."

"I know," Emily says, a silly grin in her voice. "I like it, though. It's cute, just like you. So what are you being weird about? Is everything alright at home? Have you talked to your mom lately?"

"She's texted me a few times," I say, vague.

The truth is she's texted me twice, and both times were to tell me that she found a pair of my panties somewhere and why would I leave those laying around? Well, Mom, why don't you ask your creepy boyfriend who kept trying to flirt with me and said the creepiest things when you weren't around? Seriously, that's gross. Daddy's allowed to have my panties if he wants, but I don't want some creepy dude who's dating my mom to go stealing my panties and hiding them for who even knows why. I mean, obviously I know what he's doing and I really don't even want to think about it because it makes me want to vomit. Yuck!

"Alright, so that's not it," Emily says, digging deeper. "What is it? What's wrong? I'm your best friend. You know you can tell me anything, right?"

"I know," I say. I know it's true, too. And I will. Daddy and I will tell her, I promise, just, um... not yet... "I don't know. I was talking with Daddy about college, and I really want to go, but I need to save up and figure it out."

"I'm sure he could offer you some sort of, like, um... an internship or something? Or a scholarship. They do that kind of thing there, and it's supposed to be merit-based and there's submissions and everything, but who's going to know if they fudge it a little and you win?"

"I would know," I tell her. "You and Daddy would know, too. No, I'm not doing that. I'm going to do it on my own. But I think that's why Daddy agreed. I can't go to college yet because of my mom and financial aid issues, but that doesn't mean I have to miss out on everything about college life, right? I promised Daddy I'd be a good girl, though."

Wait. Oh no! I didn't, um... I just... I didn't mean to say that! Not like that, at least. Nope...

"You told him like that?" Emily asks, a weird note in the deepest recesses of her voice. I'm really not sure what that means, and I'm scared to find out. "Did you bat your eyelashes at him, too?"

"Maybe?" I offer. I most definitely did, but I don't know where she's going with this and now I'm afraid I just screwed everything up and said something I shouldn't have.

"Well, I guess now we know why he agreed," Emily says, as if we've solved some mystery together.

"Huh? What do you mean?" I ask, acting oblivious.

"Oh, Fiona..." Emily says with a sigh. "You're so sweet and innocent. Good thing Daddy's a good person. You've got him wrapped around your finger and you don't even know it. It's kind of cute, though."

"I don't, um, it's not... it's not like that!" I say, fighting the urge to admit it all and tell her everything.

Maybe not everything, but, you know...

"When you bat your eyelashes at a guy and tell them you promise to be a good girl, well... that's like the instant win button, I think. Doesn't work all the time, but works a lot."

"Um, excuse me," I say, because turnabout is definitely fair play here. "How would you know, Emily? Little miss never had a boyfriend!"

"It's just a thing, Fiona," Emily says, like she's this wise authority on eyelash batting. "Everyone knows it. Anyways, it doesn't really matter, because you're coming. Yes!"

Which reminds me that I was also cumming earlier. Yes! This isn't an appropriate thought to have right now, is it? It was nice, though. I liked it. Daddy's good at making me cum. It's amazing.

"Are you guys staying at the usual hotel?" she asks. "You can stay in my dorm room with me that night if you want."

"Daddy said something about maybe getting a hotel that's closer to the frat house, I guess?" I say with a shrug.

"Ugh. Is he going to stand outside and chaperone us all night or something?"

"I don't think so?" I say.

I wouldn't mind, though. Can I bring a date to this? I would bring Daddy, because how fun would that be? Except, no, I can't do that because Emily will be there. Ugh. This is hard.

"I guess it's fine. I don't think he'll be too weird. Daddy's a great guy and I love him. He's honestly the best older brother ever and I'm so glad he's helping you out, too. I can see why he's worried, though. Some of the guys here at my college are kind of immature. You just have to ignore them."

"Oh," I say. I don't know what else to say.

Now I'm a little worried? I don't want to tell Emily that, though. I don't want to tell Daddy, either. I don't want him worrying and... and I'm not going to put up with anyone's stuff! Be strong and fierce, Fiona! Rawr!

I can do it.

"Oh! Before I forget, it's a costume party, sort of. It's like a masquerade theme, so everyone wears masks. There's some other games and stuff but it's sort of a secret until we get there. We don't have to do anything if we don't want to, but it could be fun. Like a speed dating thing, you know? Or date auctions and the proceeds go to one of the charities that the frat helps out. It's really cool."

"What kind of theme?" I ask. "Masks are fun, though. Sounds fancy!"

"Yup, exactly!" Emily says, excited. "It's like a naughty or nice theme. Angels and demons, kind of? Like Cupid, for Valentine's Day, or else you can be naughty and go as a demon or a succubus or something."

"Oh," I say, not so sure about that one. "Um..."

"We'll get our costumes ready the day of the party," Emily says. "We don't have to dress up a lot. They've got masks they're selling and the proceeds go to charity, too, so I'll get you one. Everyone's supposed to wear the same masks, but the ones the guys have are a little different. Those are naughty or nice themed, too."

"I'll get you a 'Nice' mask, obviously," Emily says,

giggling. "Since you told Daddy you'd be a good girl. Really, Fiona! You're so cute. I love it."

"What about you?" I ask her, awkwardly trying to avoid saying anything incriminating. I purse my lips tight shut and everything.

"I'll get a 'Naughty' one so we can go as a pair," she says. "Maybe don't tell Daddy that one. I'm not really going to be naughty or anything. It's just for fun, you know?"

"Right," I say, nodding into the phone. "Just for fun."

6

GREY

Fiona comes back downstairs smiling, but there's a hint of reluctance in her eyes, too. Yeah, look, I know she's completely naked. Trust me, I'm more than aware of this fact. That doesn't mean I don't notice the rest of her, too. Now's not the time to go screwing around and being a caveman. We can do that later.

I start to ask her what's wrong, but then I realize I should probably keep quiet. What's wrong? Isn't it obvious? She's going to a frat party with my sister. I'm kind of an expert when it comes to Fiona and Emily, and neither of them has been to a party as long as I've known them, and I've known my sister her entire life, so I'm basically an authority on this. They went to some high school dances and did whatever there, but that's it. They went to prom, too. Actual parties, though? Yeah, uh... do you even know Fiona and my sister?

I get that I have a sort of kinky fucked up relationship thing going on with Fiona at the moment, but that doesn't

35

change the fact that they're basically the "goodest girls" in the entire world, to use a term someone very special to me used recently. Mostly. Fiona has her moments, but they're reserved for me and me alone, and I'm pretty much fine with that one. Not going to hear any complaints from me.

Anyways, point being, these girls would have problems getting into trouble even if they tried. And trust me, Fiona's tried. I don't even know how she convinced me to be her cohort in supreme troublemaking here, because, uh... yeah, she's too good. Probably too good for me, which I don't like admitting.

I'm going to be good to her too, though. I'm making it my entire fucking life's mission and if anyone tries to fuck that up, well... just don't. You don't want to know what's going to happen. I'll keep Emily safe, too. Emily's just different, though. She's my sister, so her charms aren't exactly the same as Fiona's.

"Daddy?" Fiona asks, watching me from the master bathroom door.

"What's up, baby girl?" I ask her, tossing a reassuring smile her way for good measure.

"Can I have a hug before we take a shower?"

"What? Yes. Fiona, what's wrong?"

She smiles brightly as I fret and worry over her. Look, she doesn't need a reason for me to give her a hug. I'll hug this girl as much as I can. All fucking day, I don't even care. I just... I don't fucking know. I worry. I worry about a lot of stupid shit as far as Fiona's concerned, and there's plenty of times where I forget everything and just give in to the moment, but I don't think I can ever stop worrying about her.

I'm "Daddy" to her and I take this shit seriously. You have no fucking idea how much it means to her. It means a ton to me, too.

I take two strong strides and I'm at her side, standing in the doorway with her. She wraps her arms around me and hugs me tight. I blanket her in a hug, squeezing her close. We're naked, and my cock knows this, but I'm not going to let that ruin the moment.

"I wish you could come to the party with me," Fiona says, her face tight against my chest.

It has the added effect of squishing her more than adequate breasts tight against me, too. My cock twitches in response as if to say, "Pussy, please?" but I ignore it for now.

"Yeah, I don't think that one's going to fly," I say, grinning down at her. I kiss the top of her head, and when she looks up at me I kiss the tip of her nose, too. "Pretty sure Emily wouldn't be a fan, either."

"What if we told her?" Fiona asks, a flash of *something* in her eyes.

"When?" I ask, going along with this '*what if?*' scenario we're letting play out.

"Let's text her right now!"

"Right now?" I ask, laughing. "I don't know if a text will work. Seems like something we should talk with her about in person. What's gotten you so excited?"

She tosses her shoulders up into a little shrug while still hugging me tight. Basically it's the cutest fucking thing in the entire world. How the fuck are you so amazing, Fiona? I don't even know.

"I guess," she says, scrunching up her nose. "I just think it'd be fun if you could go to the party as my date."

"Not sure I can pass as a college student," I say. "I'm not saying it wouldn't be fun, though. You want to go on real dates sometime? Regular ones?"

"Is that alright?" she asks, biting her bottom lip.

"What? Yeah, of course it is, baby girl. I just... I don't know."

"You think people are going to think it's weird that we're dating," she says, reading my mind.

"That, and the fact that you call me Daddy," I say.

"I can call you Grey if you want?" she says. "In the open, I mean. Um, maybe not at yoga because I already call you Daddy there, but they know you're not my actual dad so I don't think that's a big deal."

"So, I have a real fucking mixed opinion on that," I say, probably sounding harsher than I mean to.

Fiona grins up at me, which is basically a grin that could incite a saint to do the devil's work if I ever saw one. Fuck, man. This girl...

"Why?" she asks, cute and innocent.

And that's the thing. She's cute and innocent and the sweetest girl in the world, and then somehow I end up naked in bed with her and I'm fucking the shit out of her. I don't even fucking know how this works. Seriously, no fucking clue...

"I really fucking like when you call me Daddy," I say, matter-of-fact.

"Me too," she says. "I like when you call me your good girl or baby girl, too. I want to be Daddy's good girl a lot."

"You are, baby girl," I say, bringing an immediate shining smile to her face.

"If you make me mad I'm going to call you Grey, though!" she warns, giving me a silly smirk. "Daddy's only for when you're good."

"Oh yeah?" I counter. "Well, you're only my good girl when you're good, too. And if you're bad I'm gonna spank your ass until it's red."

"Noooooo!" she pouts, making a funny face at me. "Not my butt."

"Don't worry. I'll kiss it better after."

"With your tongue?" she asks. "Between my legs? And then with your cock? On my clit, sliding it back and forth before putting it inside me?"

"Well yeah, obviously," I say, like this doesn't even need to be asked.

"Alright, but I'll do my best to be your good girl so you don't have to spank me and you can still do all of the rest of that. But you can spank me a little, alright? That's up to you, Daddy..."

"I know," I tell her, kissing her forehead. "I'll take care of you, Fiona. If you ever want to slow down or stop, let me know, though. I've got some other ideas we can try out sometime, too."

"Like the grocery store?" she asks, a greedy fire in her eyes.

"You liked that, huh?" I ask, laughing.

She nods, faster than fast. "I was going to say we could

do that for the party, but then I don't want to be like that when other people are around me but you aren't. But if we go to the party together..."

"You really want me to go to this party, huh?" I say, just stating the facts.

"I would really really like it," she says, nodding just once this time. "I know you probably can't, but maybe for another party?"

"Whoa, holy shit, you want to go to more than one party?" I ask, teasing her.

"Yup! And you're going to go with me!" she says, letting out a cute little cackle. "Mua ha ha!"

"Hey, calm down there, what kind of good girl are you?"

"I'm Daddy's good girl," she says without even thinking.

"Good answer," I say, smiling and giving her a gentle kiss on the lips. "Let's shower and get dressed."

"Can I give you a blowjob in the shower and can you cum down my throat?" she asks, as innocently as if she just asked me if I would go to church with her on Sunday.

"Fiona," I say with a growl, fighting against my inner caveman. "We need to get things done today, especially if we're going to go visit Emily for this Valentine's Day party in a couple days."

"Alright..." Fiona says, pouty. "But maybe can I give you a *really quick* blowjob in the shower? And then you cum down my throat and I swallow it all like a good girl?"

Yeah, so, this isn't my finest moment. I don't know what to tell you. What the fuck do you want me to do? I've got this perfect girl clinging to me like I'm the only man in the world, the only one she even wants to have in her world, and she's over here batting her eyelashes at me, telling me she'll be a good girl, and asking if she can give me a quick blowjob in the shower and then swallow every last drop of it.

Like I said, not my finest moment. I'm not proud of what I do, but it's done, or it's about to be done, and...

"Fast," I say, like I'm telling her she can have one cookie before dinner, but that's it.

Seriously, I'm going to Hell. I know this, but I can't seem to stop. Oh well. Fuck it.

True to her word, Fiona gives me a really quick blowjob in the shower. What the fuck was that? Three or four minutes? Who the fuck taught this girl to swallow a cock like that? I mean, I did, and... yeah, again, I'm going to Hell, probably.

Seriously, though. Holy fucking shit.

I almost forget about the fact that I told her she could go to the Valentine's Day party after that. Almost. It's only a few days, though. We'll get to that part soon, but for now I want to wash Fiona's hair. I love the way she makes this little mewling sound like she's a goddamn kitten whenever I gently massage her scalp. Her eyes close and she struggles to stand upright, gently leaning back against me or else pushing forward against the wall of the shower, just kind of wobbling back and forth like that.

Fuck. I love this girl so much. Fiona's mine in every possible way and I'm never going to let anything or anyone change that.

I just... I want her to have fun, too. I know I missed out on a lot when I was growing up. I needed to take care of Emily. I don't regret it. My sister is the only close family I have left and I wouldn't give that up for the world. Maybe I didn't get the standard "new adult" college or life experiences that other people had, but I did my best.

Fiona doesn't have those same restrictions and I refuse to force her into them. That doesn't mean I'm going to give her up. I tried to fucking tell her to go live her life, and she just clung to me tighter, so what the fuck do you want me to do? She wants to do this, though. She wants to go to this college party, and go to college, and I have no fucking clue what else.

We'll figure it out. Together. I'll be here to protect her, no matter what. I'll always be there.

I promise.

FIONA

"Whoa."

Seriously, this is a really "whoa" moment for me. Daddy and I usually stay in this nice business hotel when we come to visit Emily. It's about an hour or two away from home, depending on the traffic, and the business hotel is nice. I thought that business hotels meant that you could only stay there if you were there for business, but the first time I told Daddy that and when I asked him if it was alright for me to be there--because I definitely wasn't doing any business--he gave me a funny look and laughed.

"That's just what they call them," he told me. "No clue why. Usually they've got rooms you can use for meetings, but to be honest basically every hotel has meeting rooms now. Some have more than others, or some have bigger common areas by the lobby that are good for meetings. That's why this is considered a business hotel. See?"

He gestured to the area by the lobby where they had a

gas fireplace set up in the middle with some bookshelves and books to look fancier and more businessy, I guess? Plus a lot of chairs for sitting, because apparently business people don't like to stand. And, the thing that I learned later, they purposefully put the bar near the common sitting area so you can get a drink while you're there.

Apparently business sometimes involves a lot of alcohol. Or a little alcohol. I don't really know and I'm not old enough to drink, so I'm not sure I'm going to learn anytime soon. Daddy accepts many things, but I don't think he wants me to do any underage drinking. We need to be responsible together. I don't mind, either. I actually really like that about him. I think it's fun.

Anyways, that's the business hotel we usually stay at, but, um... so that one is maybe too far away from the Sigma Epsilon Chi frat house. Daddy found this other hotel only a few blocks away, right by the big river that splits Emily's college town in half. We've never been over here and I didn't even realize it was a hotel at first until we pulled in and handed the car off to the valet.

"What do you think?" Daddy asks, grinning like a foolish idiot.

Not just a fool or an idiot, but both. I think I'm doing the same, but maybe I'm just gaping.

And, um... so this happened before, which led to where we are now...

"I see you have Platinum status with us, sir," the woman at the front desk says to him. "And you usually stay in one of our other hotels when you visit. Looks like you come into town often?"

"Yeah, we're just visiting," he tells her. "Fiona wanted to check out colleges in the area with my little sister, and this one was closer, so..."

The woman smiles at him and winks in a way I really don't like. Daddy's mine! Also I think she thinks that I'm his daughter or something? I mean, it's probably not the first time this has happened. Daddy's not exactly old at the super handsome age of thirty, but people are just dumb and I guess it doesn't help that I call him Daddy all the time.

Whatever, bitch! He's my Daddy and you can't have him!

I don't say that. That would be rude and Daddy would probably spank me once we get to the room, but I glare at her when he's not looking and I think she grows even more interested in him after that. Ugh!

"As one of our valued Platinum members, and because I hope you'll considering staying here again on one of your future trips to visit your little sister, how about I give you a room upgrade?"

Which, you know, room upgrade. What's a room upgrade? I'm sort of out of the loop here and I know this maybe sounds dumb but I don't understand what's going on.

"And if you need *anything*," the woman says before handing us the keys. "*Anything at all*, Mr. Royal, I will be happy to *personally* assist you. Possibly while your little sister shows your daughter around campus?"

I'm about to cut a bitch, or more specifically this bitch, except before I can Daddy drags me away, nods politely to the woman at the front desk, and pulls me over to the elevators. I grumble and pout and probably look super grumpy the entire ride up.

"You're mine," I tell him, mumbling in the elevator.

"I know," Daddy says.

"Stop laughing!" I snap.

"I'm not laughing!" he says, but then he does. He laughs! I just saw it and I heard it!

"Daddy! You said you weren't laughing!"

"Look, I don't even--"

Except then he takes out our key card to open the door to our room and out slides a personalized business card. It falls to the floor and I pick it up and stare at it.

It's hers!

It's not even a business card, either. Not a real one. It's just a card with a handwritten number and name on it. Her name, her number.

"I'm gonna fight her!" I say, ready to stomp down the hall with this card. I may be small, but I'm feisty! Fuck you, lady.

Daddy grabs the back of my shirt like we're in some kind of cartoon and I can't even stomp down the hall and fight her now. Ugh!

"You're not going to fight her," he says, shaking his head. "I'm going to throw the card away. Obviously I'm not calling her, Fiona."

"You could get lonely," I say, pouting. "You might get lonely and you'll miss me and then you'll see the card in the trash and you'll call her and then I'll be sad."

"Fiona, I'm not going to do that."

"Yeah but I don't like her," I tell him.

And that's, um... that's what we do, except then Daddy opens the door to our room and...

"Whoa," I say.

"Yeah, uh..."

Daddy and I stand at the entrance to our room, just through the doorway. The door slowly closes behind us as we gape and stare at whatever this is. I don't even know? This is a hotel room? It's bigger than the apartment I used to live in with my mom.

"I don't know what this is," I say, trying to figure out what words are and how to use them to explain things.

"According to this, uh... we're in the Ebersol Suite?" Daddy says, staring at the little packet that our keycards came in.

He hands me mine, because he always gets an extra one for me. I like to save them and write little notes on them to remember the dates when Daddy and I went to the hotel together. I mean, it's usually the same hotel most of the time, but it's still fun to remember. And who knows when we'll go to new hotels? Like this one.

I don't even know if this is a hotel, though. It's like an alternate dimension.

We walk into the bedroom of our suite, which is like some giant hallway with a bed at one end, an office area with a desk set up at the other, and a giant TV in the middle opposite the bed. The bed might as well be two beds, that's how big it is. Daddy's bed back home is plenty big for the two of us, but this bed is probably big enough for, like... four of us? I don't want four of us, though. I like having just two of us.

"Uh, Fiona?" Daddy says, standing by the floor to ceiling windows at one end of the bedroom hallway room thing whatever.

"Yes, Daddy?" I answer.

One of those windows isn't a window. Daddy twists a latch, grabs the handle, and pushes the glass door. It opens onto a super cute and amazing balcony with a little table and a pair of chairs. The balcony overlooks the river and I have a sneaking suspicion it offers a beautiful view of the sunset in the evening.

"Whoa," I say, stepping out onto the balcony with him.

"Yeah, uh..." he says, his head bobbing in a quiet nod every few seconds.

"Daddy?" I ask.

"Yes?"

"Can we have sex on the balcony?" I promise this is a serious question. Have you seen this balcony?

"Yeah, uh, no," he says. "Not going to happen."

"What's even the point of a balcony like this if you can't have sex on it?" I counter.

Again, I swear this is a serious question! This balcony is just begging for Daddy to strip me naked, force my hands onto the balcony railing, smack my ass a few times, and then slide his throbbing hot cock into my ready and waiting little pussy. And we can do that while watching the sunset! Oh my gosh.

"It's..." Daddy stumbles for words, trying to come up

with an answer to my balcony question. "Just get your ass inside."

"Or what?" I ask.

I've never wanted to be naughty more than I do at this very moment. I'm sorry, Daddy. I'm supposed to be a good girl for you but it's way too hard right now.

"Or I won't have sex with you for a week," he says, ending all of my fantasies of being pleasantly punished.

"Noooooooo!" I cry, fleeing the balcony.

Daddy snickers at me and shuts the glass door behind us, then twists the latch to lock it. I stand by the bed, obedient, hands crossed in front of me.

"I'm good," I tell him. "Promise. I'm your good girl. Please."

"Please what?" he asks, teasing me and smirking, but trying to be strong and disciplinary.

"Please have sex with me?" I suggest.

"Where?" he asks.

"On the--" I stop when his eyes flash and he gives me a mischievous grin. "Not on the balcony!"

"Good girl," he says, coming close and kissing the top of my head. "Let's check out the rest of the room. I'm sure there's plenty of other places you'll like."

I mean, maybe, but the balcony just seems so great. A great balcony is hard to come by. I think they are, at least. Daddy and I have no balconies back home, and I've never had a balcony in any of the apartments I lived in with my mom when I was growing up. I have seen and heard of balconies, but I have had rare occasion to actually be on a balcony.

What if I never see a balcony ever again? What if this is my only chance, the only time, and then for the rest of my life I...

"Whoa," I say.

"Yeah, uh..." Daddy says.

"This is a bathroom?" I ask.

"I guess so?" he says.

The bathroom is basically as big as Daddy's bedroom back home, and considering he has the master bedroom, um... that's big. I don't think any bathroom has a right to be this big, but here this one is, being big.

A double vanity sits right in the middle. This is the elusive "His" and "Hers" sink set up I've heard about. I think. I don't actually know, but what else do you even do with two sinks in a bathroom? The toilet is a toilet. Nobody cares about toilets. And then there's a shower, which is huge, with glass surrounding it on all sides.

I don't care about those parts, though. The part I care about is the bathtub, or hot tub, or whatever this thing is. It's a big tub and it's got some controls on the side which look like they could be used to great effect to make magical things happen when you fill it up. A giant faucet rests on the side in the middle, with knobs for hot and cold water.

Daddy leans over the tub and pushes open the wooden slatted doors. We see the bedroom on the other side, and then way at the other end we see a picture perfect view of the balcony.

"So you can see the sunset while you're in the hot tub?"

I ask, because this is a question that needs asking right at this very moment.

"It's a whirlpool bathtub," Daddy says, grinning at me. "Kind of a mix between a hot tub and a bathtub. We can turn on the jets and bubbles with this remote panel. Looks like we can watch the sunset while we're soaking in the tub, yes."

And then, you know, as you do, I ask:

"Can we have sex in the hot tub?"

Daddy grins at me, wicked and delicious.

Mmm yum!

.

8

GREY

As much as I would love to turn on the water, strip Fiona bare, and kiss every inch of her tight little body while we waited for the tub to fill up, I need to actually get some work done. And she needs to meet up with Emily so they can go pick out their outfits for tonight's party, too.

I have no idea what kind of party this is. Who needs outfits for a Valentine's Day party? What the hell, this isn't Halloween, people. It's probably just some frat thing. Like toga parties or whatever? Does anyone still do that?

Wait. Fuck. I really don't like the idea of Fiona and Emily showing up to a party in... a white sheet. What the fuck do people wear under their togas? Clothes or something, I hope, except seriously why the fuck would anyone wear clothes under a toga? I'm doing some serious wishful thinking right here and my mind and body are at odds with one another.

On the one hand, these girls need to *not* go walking around some frat party wearing only a white sheet. That's just asking for trouble. On the other hand, I would definitely be down for Fiona walking around the house wearing a sheet when it's just her and I. I mean, fuck it, she can walk around naked if she wants. Which she does sometimes, and basically I'm the luckiest man in the world.

Fiona's just... I don't even fucking know. How do I describe the best thing that's ever happened to me? There's literally nothing I can compare her to that would even come close to explaining how sexy, amazing, beautiful, fuckable, cute, erotic, arousing...

Too many words and I don't have time for this shit. I'm going to a business meeting while Fiona and Emily get outfits for the party, whatever the hell that entails.

I decide to walk since the rendez-vous point is pretty close to the hotel we're staying at. I set up an impromptu meeting with a man my company's done business with for a long time now. He actually knew my parents and I met him a few times when I was younger. He's a nice guy, and...

He brought his dickhead of a son with him. Fuck.

The worst part is I can't exactly say anything, you know? You've just got to grin and bear it in situations like this, which is pretty fucking annoying, but oh well. I can deal with it. We aren't here to discuss anything that important, so this shouldn't last long. He's only here as a favor to me because I thought it'd be best if I made this into an actual business trip instead of simply stealing Fiona away to some luxury hotel and getting asked all sorts of questions afterwards.

It's hard enough as it is. Some people get it, and other people, well... they wonder why I have some pert little eighteen year old girl living in my house with me. I don't know. What do you want me to say? I like spanking her ass and she likes calling me Daddy, and we both fit together perfectly so we fuck a lot? Plus cuddling and everything. This is the whole package, and I'm not talking one of those tiny packages you get where you wonder if it was even worth it for the company to ship you a box the size of a can of soup.

Anyways, fuck it, I'm here.

Jameson stands and holds out his hand. I accept it and shake, firm. This is our businessman's code right here. Who needs secret handshakes when you can just stick to a strong one? It says exactly what needs to be said.

His son, Charles, just kind of waves and says, "Hey, Grey."

"Grey," Jameson says with a nod. "You know my son. I thought it would be a good idea to have him tag along today. He's just started college and he'll be taking over for me some day, so I wanted to get him involved even if we won't be going over anything that detailed."

"Charles," I say, offering the kid a curt smile. "It's been awhile, buddy. Hope everything's going well." To Jameson, I add, "I completely understand what you mean. I was basically thrown under the bus and to the wolves at the same time when I first took over, so getting the next generation acclimated sooner instead of later is always a good idea."

"Right," Jameson says with a grin, like he's glad that I agree. "Actually, I think Charles goes to the same college as your sister."

"Yeah," Charles says, also with a grin, but his grin is annoying as fuck and I want to punch him. "She's probably going to the Valentine's Day party me and my brothers are throwing. The Sigma Epsilon Chi frat parties are epic."

Yeah, well, now I want to punch him even more. I could use a drink first, though. Good thing we're in a brewery restaurant. There should be plenty to go around.

"Sigma Epsilon Chi does some fine work in the community," Jameson says, ignoring his son's focus on the party. "We can talk about that later, though. Shall we order appetizers and a few drinks and get right into it? You don't have any time constraints, right, Grey?"

And this is when I realize I made some kind of fatal mistake. I don't know how it happened. It's probably my own damn fault, though. I set this up as a last minute meeting, but that also means I obviously have nothing else going on today. Jameson loves to talk, too. Usually it's not so bad because whenever I'm with him we're in a decent sized group of people and it's not that hard to make some excuse and head out early.

I have no excuses this time. I've got no one else I can leave him with while he tells me about his glory days. And as if that's not bad enough, I've got to somehow mentally deal with the fact that Charles is going to be at the same party as Emily and Fiona.

Fuck.

9

FIONA

"Um, Emily? I really don't know about this. I don't think Daddy would like it."

This isn't *entirely* accurate. I'm sure Daddy would *love* if he saw me wearing this. For just us. Or maybe if I was with him and the two of us were going on a date? That would be really fun! And then everyone would see me with Daddy and they'd know I was his, because this is the kind of dress that makes men like Daddy turn into cavemen that are super protective and possessive.

I've never worn a dress like this around him before, so I'm just kind of guessing at the moment, but... just saying, I'm pretty sure I know what I'm talking about when it comes to how Daddy will feel about this dress.

"Oh, pft!" Emily says, dismissive. "That dress is amazing. You look hot, Fiona. What Daddy doesn't know won't hurt him, and it's not like we're doing anything, you know? We're just going to a party and then we'll change after we leave. He'll never know."

"I guess..." I say, but I don't. I don't guess!

"Anyways, you have to wear it," Emily adds. "We match! This'll be so much fun."

I awkwardly shuffle out of the dressing room at Emily's urging and we stand in front of a huge wall mirror. To be fair, I do look pretty hot. Emily also looks hot. We're both hot, which is... it's different and fun and I've never really worn anything like this before, but that's also why I'm so worried.

I really doubt Daddy expects us to go to the party like this. If I had to guess, he thinks we'll be wearing a cute pair of jeans and maybe a nice, modest sweater. The sweater can have a little bit of a v-neck to show, like... the tiniest amount of cleavage. Just a super tiny small little bit, but that's it! It's February so it's sort of cold out and honestly I like wearing warm clothes because the cold is too cold for me.

This is also why I think I will really like soaking in the hot tub with Daddy. I know it's not a real hot tub, but it'll be nice and cozy and warm and we'll be naked and he can make me even warmer, and...

Please, Daddy!

My mind wanders to the moment before he's about to make me cum in my imaginary setting of us soaking in the hot tub in our super fancy room together. And we're going to do that! We'll do it for real. I'll be such a good girl and Daddy will be so nice to me, and it'll basically be amazing.

Except maybe not if I go to the party in this dress. Ugh!

"Let's spin around," Emily says, kind of spinning me before she even finishes talking.

I look over my shoulder at the mirror, and Emily does, too.

"Aw yeah, that's what I'm talking about!" she says, giddy. "Fiona, this is amazing."

"What is?" I ask.

"Look at our butts, girl," Emily says, all sassy and confident.

I look, and... yup, our butts are amazing. What the heck! I'm sorry, Daddy! I'm so so sorry I have an amazing butt right now!

One time, or, um... alright, so it was a lot of times but this was the first time! Anyways, one time I borrowed Emily's yoga pants. She's a little smaller than me, but her clothes still mostly fit me. These are yoga pants, though, so they're extra tight, and what happens when you wear extra tight clothes that are already supposed to be tight is, well... it really shows off everything. And I literally mean everything.

Which was kind of fine, because we were just doing yoga at home with Grey. Who I had a crush on. And he was behind me the entire time, getting a perfect view of my ass and everything in between. This was before Daddy had seen me without any of my clothes on at all, which was exhilarating and exciting and...

That's a different story, but the point is that this dress really isn't any better. It's not yoga pants, so I'm not showing off everything and then some, but the fabric follows my curves perfectly until it drops off around the middle of my thigh. Basically this dress is perfect for swaying my hips side to side and making men stupid as they watch my butt bounce while they fall under my spell.

But I don't want them to fall under my spell! I want Daddy to, but he already has, except I kind of want him to do it again and again? I have a lot of spells, some I probably don't even know about yet, and I want Daddy to fall under all of them.

And, you know, besides our now perfect butts, these dresses just aren't very good. These are not the kind of dresses that a good girl wears.

They're simple, so at least there's that. Emily picked out two matching tube dresses for the both of us; her with red to be naughty, and me with a white one because I'm nice. Except, you know, our butts are just showing everything off, and there's no straps so our cleavage isn't exactly hidden away, either. The dresses cling to our hips, shaping us into as close to an hourglass figure as anyone will ever get.

"We need shoes!" Emily says, excitedly running away from the changing room.

"Emily!" I yell after her, because seriously these aren't the kinds of dresses you should run around in. Boobs are just going to fall out and end up all over the place, and...

It's like an old slow motion beach scene on a TV show where the girl in a bathing suit runs on the beach, everything bouncing all over the place, except instead of captivating viewers I'm pretty sure Daddy's going to kill us. I'm not running, Daddy! I'm being good! I'm being as good as I can be, at least. I grab our clothes and purses from the changing room and slowly waddle over to Emily and the shoes. I go slow, no bouncing whatsoever. I mean, there's probably a little bouncing, but I'm trying really hard not to bounce.

I'm Daddy's good girl, dammit! Ugh!

"What if we swap colors for our shoes?" Emily suggests, holding out a red pair of "fuck me" platform pumps.

I dump all of our clothes and stuff onto a bench and daintily accept the shoes, just kind of staring at them. Because, yup, I really don't think this is a good idea. These are the kind of heels I would wear if I just wanted Daddy to look at me and fuck my brains out immediately without even thinking about it.

I feel like this is saying a lot, because seriously Daddy's very good with being patient and having will power. If a pair of shoes can make him go crazy, everyone else is going to go insane.

"Emily, I--" I start to say, but she's already trying her pair of white platform pumps.

Her in a red dress with white pumps, and me in a white dress with red pumps. If this isn't the worst idea ever, I don't know what is.

"We're so fucking hot," Emily says, strutting her stuff.

I mean, it's true... I didn't think my butt could look any better, but these shoes are doing some sort of curvy magic or something. Who knew doing yoga and wearing a form-fitting tube dress and the right kind of shoes could make your legs look like something out of a porno?

These legs are for Daddy only, though! Dammit, Emily!

"Yeah, we definitely can't let Daddy find out about this," she says.

"Maybe we should get--"

She cuts me off before I can suggest we get something else. Dragging me back to the dressing room, Emily takes her regular clothes and purse and hurries inside to change. I just kind of stand there, legs wobbling like I'm some sort of baby deer or I don't know.

Before I head into the changing room to get back to normal, I spot a guy who works here staring at my butt. He doesn't even try to hide it, but he's also walking around and trying to pretend like he's working. Before I can say anything, he walks face first into a column rising up near the entrance to the changing area.

See, Emily? Do you see this? This is why we shouldn't wear dresses and shoes like this! I'm not even making this up. It's dangerous. Someone's going to get hurt.

Also, Daddy's going to kill us. My butt's going to be so red once he's done with me. I don't even want to know what kind of punishment he comes up with after that. I don't think spanking will be enough for this one.

I'm sorry, Daddy!

GREY

Business is over, but we're still at the brewery. I've lost count of how many drinks Jameson and I have had. That's not to say I'm drinking most of them, because I'm not. I've stuck to one an hour the entire time, and even then I'm really nursing this current beer. I tried to sneak in something non-alcoholic at one point, but Jameson just laughed it off like it was a joke and ordered me a banana bread flavored stout that they make locally.

I mean, look, the stout's great. I love stout and porter, and usually the darker the beer the better. Not that I'm a huge drinker, but business and pleasure tend to blur lines sometimes and I like to enjoy myself when I go out.

"Show Charles the picture from that trust building exercise you did at your company picnic a couple years ago!" Jameson booms, laughing over his beer. He definitely hasn't kept to the one beer an hour rule I'm holding myself to. Maybe double that, if we're being conservative.

Charles is old enough to drink, too. He orders these

hipster IPAs and they smell more like a grassy field than a beer but to each their own. I like the smell of hops every now and then, but the IPA craze is a little too much for me.

I pull out my phone to show off the obligatory picture. I'm hoping we can wind this down soon and I can get out of here. Maybe secretly text Fiona, see how things are, make sure her and Emily are doing fine. I'm not going to text Emily, because then she'll be on high alert and start bugging Fiona and asking if I texted her, too.

Is he texting you, Fifi? I can just hear it now. My sister is a lot to handle. I should know considering I've had to deal with her my entire life.

I scan through my pictures, grateful that I've never taken any involving my steamy escapades with Fiona. Trust me, I've wanted to. Her pussy belongs in an art gallery and it should probably be discussed in every major art class in colleges worldwide, that's how aesthetically perfect it is.

And if you think that's perfect, imagine seeing it painted with my cum, inside and out, her pussy lips red and sore from being fucked into submission by my cock, so puffy and tight that I can barely pull out after we're done, that's how hard she's been clenching down on my shaft the entire time.

Yeah, I'd frame that. If I ever become some sort of famous photographer, that'll be my masterpiece.

Thankfully there's nothing like that on my phone right now, especially since Jameson and Charles are adamant about doing the whole "sharing is caring" storytime fun and they keep glancing over to see if I've found the picture yet. I finally find the picture he's talking about, which is just me and Emily and Fiona standing with a bunch of the guys and girls who work with me. It's a group photo, and I guess I never realized it until now, but, uh... yeah.. this might not be as innocent as I thought.

It was a trust building exercise for fuck's sake! It wasn't supposed to be sexy. Holy shit.

We put on harnesses and did this ropes course twenty feet in the air. At the end, everyone had to do a drop off, just straight down, except a few feet after you started to free fall you hit this other part that sent you into a fifty foot zip line glide.

I guess I never realized until now that the harnesses were, uh... yeah, so basically they prop up Emily and Fiona's breasts and also dig into their shorts, giving them an obvious frontal wedgie. This isn't even close to the same as that one time Fiona wore Emily's yoga pants and had the perfect camel toe, but it's not that much better, either.

Jameson laughs, showing the picture off to his son. "This was a hoot! I love Grey's ideas for company events. You really bring life and passion back into this business, young man. We started doing the same with my company, but it's still gaining ground. Everyone likes it so far."

Apparently Charles likes it a little too much. "Who's that?" he asks, pointing to Fiona.

"Ah, yes, it's nice what you're doing for her, Grey," Jameson adds with a old man's gentle smile. "It's very nice."

"That's..." What I really want to say is if he doesn't stop

eye-fucking her that's the reason I'm going to rip his throat out, but instead I finish with, "Fiona. She's Emily's best friend."

And mine. Not my friend. Just mine. Fiona is all mine.

"Your sister, right?" Charles asks. "Does Fiona go to college around here, too?"

"No," I say, full stop. There's a lot of shit I'm saying no to right now, but we won't get into that.

"She's here though, right?" Jameson asks. "I think you mentioned she was going to go to a party with Emily and that's why you wanted to set up this short notice meeting between the two of us?"

Holy fucking shit, man! You're killing me here.

Also, Charles gets this look in his eyes. It's the kind of look I know very well, because it's probably the kind of look I have in my eyes every time I look at Fiona. Except this fuckface better not even try to look at her. No part of her. Don't even fucking look at her fingernail or I'll--

"I've got to go," Charles says, standing. "Thanks for having me sit in on this business meeting, Dad. Grey, it was nice seeing you again. I'll keep an eye out for Emily and Fiona at the Sigma Epsilon Chi party. Don't worry, I'll make sure they're taken *very* good care of. I'm sure the *whole frat* would be more than happy to take care of them and make sure they have a great time. I'm definitely interested in meeting Fiona. I'll tell her you said hi."

Yeah, this kid's dead. I'm going to jail for murder. Is it still technically serial murder if I kill every single Sigma Epsilon Chi frat member all at once?

"Oh, those boys," Jameson says with a laugh. "I'm sure

they'll treat the girls nice, though. They do so many good things for the community."

"Yeah," I say, blunt. "I'm sure."

I'm about to make some excuse for why I have to leave right now at this exact moment. The real reason is I'm going to hunt down Emily and Fiona and lock both their asses in my hotel room until the party's over. No fucking way in hell am I letting my sister and Fiona go to some fucking gangbang orgy S.E.X. party. Not even one fucking ounce of sex is happening, and don't even try to fucking ask me what an ounce of sex is. I don't know and I don't care, but it's not happening.

No one's getting fucked tonight. I'll cockblock every-one. I'll even cockblock myself if I have to. Don't even fucking try me.

That's my mental state at the moment. I don't even want to try and explain how it changes when Jameson calls over our waitress and orders a full flight of local beer for each of us.

"Might as well try them all while we're here!" he says, holding up his current glass before downing it in one last swig. "Do you want to split some nachos, Grey? I don't know why, but I'm really in the mood for nachos all of a sudden."

I hate the world right now.

FIONA

I don't even recognize myself, which is kind of saying a lot considering I've seen myself basically every day of my entire life. The girl in Emily's dorm room mirror can't possibly be me, but, um... I'm standing in front of it, so...

"Whoa!" Emily says, grinning wide at me.

"Yeah, um..." I say, moving a little side to side and watching the girl in the mirror move the exact same way.

Seriously, though, is that me? Because, oh my gosh, I'm super fucking hot right now. I want to show Daddy. Also I don't want to show Daddy. Daddy's going to punish me so much if I go out like this, but if I was alone with Daddy and I looked like this what would he do to me?

There's two sides to this and I don't know how either will go.

I flip up the thin white mask Emily gave me. The masks act as our tickets into the party, I guess. No one else is allowed in, and we need to keep our masks on at all times. No name tags, and I guess we're not even supposed to ask each other our real names? I don't quite understand the point of that, and this is supposed to be a single's party, so, um...

I'm not single? I'm with Daddy, duh. Except we haven't told Emily that and we haven't told anyone that, and...

I don't like this. I'm feeling really self-conscious right about now and I wish I could just go back to the hotel and soak in a hot and steamy bubble bath. Daddy and I don't even have to have sex. We can just lay together and cuddle with the bubbles and he likes when I massage his hands for him.

I like that, too. I like to run my fingers across each vein and tendon in his hand as I rub them. I like to squeeze the muscle between his thumb and index finger, and then gently massage the underside of his wrist. Don't forget each of his fingertips! Daddy likes when I squeeze them gently and slowly in a circle.

I'm a very good girl, Daddy. Promise.

Except here I am wearing some slinky white tube dress with a pair of "fuck me" red platform pumps and a simple white mask with a little feather sticking out of the left side. The only thing I recognize when I looked in the mirror are my eyes. It's like the rest of me suddenly belongs to an entirely different girl or something.

Emily pulls off a similar transformation act. When she dons the mask, she starts doing this little sashay around her room, side to side. Ba-dum-shh, ba-dum-shh, her hips swaying to some silent sexy beat.

"I think this is a little too much," I tell her, trying to be the voice of reason.

"Oh, pft!" Emily says, with a snooty fake laugh. "It's a masquerade party, Fiona. That's half the fun. We get to pretend like we're some sort of dropdead gorgeous bomb-shells and we do this all the time, but no one will ever know it's us."

"I don't know..." I say, slow. "I don't think Daddy's going to be very happy about this."

"Well, we're not going to tell him, obviously," Emily says with a shrug. "Seriously though, nothing's going to happen. It's a big party so there'll be tons of people there. We'll stay in the main room and we'll stick together so we don't end up in a bad situation. Easy peasy!"

I mean... her idea does have a certain allure to it. I don't like admitting that, but it's not like Emily and I are going to do anything bad, right? We'll be together so that means we're safer, and also it's in a frat house, so there's going to be older and more responsible college students there? I've visited Emily at college a bunch of times when Daddy comes here for the weekend or on business, and it never seems like it's the kind of place where really bad things happen.

Yes, I'm dressed in what most people would probably call a slutty outfit, but...

- **a)** I'm not a slut.

- **b)** No one's going to know who I am.

I'm going to save these clothes, too. The shoes, the

dress, and the mask. And one day when Daddy least expects it...

Kaboom!

Surprise, Daddy! I'm a bombshell. Fuck me, please? I love you...

"Are you going to wear panties with your dress?" Emily asks, glancing towards my butt.

"What! Yes? Emily, we can't just walk into a party without panties on," I tell her.

"I just meant, um... you know... there's going to be panty lines. Especially with a white dress. People might be able to see them, too? Like, what if someone spills a drink on your back? Or front. Either one probably wouldn't be good."

"Well, I need to wear panties," I say. I'm sticking to this one.

"What about a thong?" Emily asks.

"I didn't bring one," I tell her.

I don't tell her that Daddy helped me pack and if I did bring I thong I would have left it at the hotel room so I could wear it for him later.

"I've got one! You can borrow it. It's new. I haven't worn it yet, so you can just keep it."

Emily fishes through the panty drawer in her dresser and pulls out this cute little thong. Major emphasis on little, but it's still pretty cute. It's lacy and white and it would go really well with my dress. It even has the price tag still attached.

I just, um...

"Oh, let's take a picture and put it on Snapchat!" Emily says, jumping away after handing me the thong.

She snatches her phone from her purse and hurries back to me.

"Um," I say, caught off guard.

"One selfie with both of us, and then I'll take your picture and you take mine, alright?"

"Um!"

Snap. There's a selfie. Well then!

And then she jumps away from me and plays photographer. "Pose for the camera, Fifi," she says.

I put my hands on my hips and lift one foot a little, resting on the toe of my pumps. Then I stick my tongue out at her. She grins and snaps a picture.

"I posted it on Snapchat," she says. "I'll send you a copy, too. Do me now?"

"Posted it on Snapchat to who?" I ask, absent-mindedly taking her phone.

Emily does this sexy pose for me and I take her picture. She comes over and shows me where to post it, clicking through everything for me.

"Um, that's not a person," I tell her, scrunching up my nose.

"Nope!" she says, giggling. "That's the local school Snapchat. Anyone who's here will be able to see it. It'll add to the mystery. We're hyping ourselves up for the party. People will be looking for us now. Cool, right?"

"So basically everyone who goes to your school can see this?" I ask, my face turning whiter than my dress.

"Well, not *everyone*," she says, and I start to breath a sigh of relief. It doesn't come, though. "Only people with Snapchat can see it," she adds. "The teachers probably won't have it."

I know we're going to a party and people will see us like this. That's not a picture, though! That's just a party. Maybe people will take pictures there, but I was kind of hoping to avoid that altogether and just lay low and be a good girl and have some fun and...

And now everyone can see a picture of me. Snapchat is temporary, but they can take screenshots or whatever, plus I think the local ones last longer so you can look at them over and over again for awhile. I don't know.

I got Snapchat to tease Daddy and because Emily begged me to. I don't really use it. I haven't even used it to tease Daddy yet.

But now a sexy picture of me in my incredibly over the top sultry outfit is on there for everyone to see.

I'm dead.

12

GREY

I have some serious business relationships with Jameson that I can't jeopardize by randomly ditching him. There, I said it.

Also, hell if I care about that right now. I'm making plans to excuse myself to the bathroom, quietly pay my tab at the bar when he's not looking, and make my great escape. I'm not exactly proud of that one, and he'll probably give me shit for it later, but whatever.

Why did I ever agree to let Fiona go to this party? I know why, and my intentions were good. So were hers. We had good intentions, but baby girl, there's no fucking way we can let this happen anymore. I'm sorry.

The worst part is she's probably already there, so I've got to make even more plans. How do I come up with a plausible reason for why I need to drag Emily and Fiona out of a frat house during a Valentine's Day party? This is a tough one, but honestly I think I can just "I'm a parent" my way out of this one. It works like a charm with most college kids. Tell them you're a parent and they immediately freeze and try to pretend they aren't doing something they don't want their parents knowing about.

The plan has no finesse, but it gets the job done, and that's what's important at the moment.

I don't even get spring my plan into action, because as soon as I move to stand up and excuse myself to go to the restroom, a woman who is dressed to kill, and wearing high heels that could probably do exactly that, sits down next to me and wraps her hands around my arm.

"Well, well, well," she says, her sultry voice licking at my ear. "Mr. Grey Royal. I do believe I told you to let me know if you were free and in need of company for the evening..."

It's the fucking front desk woman. The one who slipped me her name and number, and the one who Fiona wanted to stomp back to the lobby so she could fight. I mean, who knows, maybe I should have let Fiona fight her, except, uh... yeah, like I just said this woman is dressed to kill and I don't know if Fiona could kill a fly.

Fiona would try really hard, though. That's the important part. Going to be honest, the fact that she probably can't beat anyone up isn't exactly a negative in my book. I'm pretty much fine with it, actually. I do like when she's cute and feisty, though.

"Oh ho ho," Jameson says, cheeks red from our ongoing drinking session. "You have a friend, Grey! How long's this been going on?"

"Hopefully it'll be going on all night," the woman says,

flashing Jameson a wink. "He's got the perfect hotel room for it."

"Jameson," I say, mostly ignoring the fact that this woman is tracing my bicep with her fingers. "This is..."

No fucking clue. Who the hell is she again? She's the front desk woman. That's all I know.

"Holly," she says, holding out one hand to shake Jameson's while the other stays firmly attached to my muscular arm. "Grey and I just met today, but I think we're going to be *very* good friends soon enough."

"That's not the kind of offer you can turn down," Jameson says, grinning at me. "I suppose this means we should part ways for the evening. We'll hammer out the final details before the end of the week, Grey. It's always good doing business with you."

Jameson waves the waitress over and hands her his credit card without even seeing the bill.

"Don't worry," he adds with a wink. "I'll get this one. You and your new lady friend go have fun. Sounds like you're in for an interesting night."

Holly takes this to mean she's got me all to herself and stands up so she can drag me off into the night or something. This isn't how I had planned on ditching Jameson, but, uh, yeah... what the hell? Sure. It works.

We get outside and Holly tries to hold my hand as we walk back to the hotel.

"Yeah, uh, no?" I say, and then because I'm not a completely heartless and rude asshole, I add, "No thanks."

Holly laughs and peeks over at me with a sultry smirk. "You don't have to pay if that's what you're thinking. I'm not that kind of girl. Even if I was, you'd be completely free, sugar."

"Look, uh… seriously, I'm flattered and all, and you're obviously an attractive woman, but--"

My phone interrupts me. It buzzes quick and my mind immediately flashes to there somehow being trouble. Who's in trouble? Fiona and Emily? Fuck! I'll kill someone. I will fight as many people as I have to and…

I check my notifications and I've got… nothing.

No texts, at least. There's something from Snapchat, which I don't really understand. It's for taking pictures, but they go away after a certain amount of time? Fiona explained it to me, and I sort of get it, but it's like…

"So you're saying I can send you a dick pic and it'll vanish after a few seconds?" I asked her.

"Daddy!" Fiona said, slapping my shoulder and laughing, but her cheeks turned redder than a stop sign, too. "I mean, you *can*…"

And she can send me sexy pictures, too. Completely safe or something, except when it's not and someone screenshots your pictures, so, uh… yeah, it's not completely safe at all. Still sounded fun and I'm not going to abuse Fiona's trust. I doubt she'd start spreading pictures of my cock over the worldwide web either, but we haven't even gotten to that part yet.

We took a picture of the two of us with dog ears and when we opened our mouths this cartoon dog tongue came out and licked at the screen. That's about it.

Emily has Snapchat too and she just takes pictures of her with an angel halo or whatever the fuck. Goddess leaf tiara? Seriously, who the fuck comes up with this shit? Fuck if I know.

I'm about to just pocket my phone and figure out a way to ditch Holly the same as I was going to ditch Jameson, but she sees the Snapchat notification and laughs.

"Tonight's going to be a fun night," she says, nodding towards my phone. "Whenever there's a big party going on, the college kids post a ton of pictures to the local Snapchat. It gets crazy. They think they're safe because the pictures go away after awhile. Kind of like how what happens in Vegas stays in Vegas, but this ain't Vegas, let me tell you..."

"Yeah?" I ask, my heart about to burst out of my chest and skydive down a volcano into the deepest depths of the earth. "Like what?"

"Sometimes it's harmless. Just kids having fun, doing silly things. Sometimes it's more like all the reasons parents worry about their kids going away to college. There's definitely been some porn star moments every now and then. Everything's off Snapchat after twenty-four hours, but you never know if someone's going to make a copy. Everyone forgets that part. It's one of those unspoken rules that no one will do it, but no one ever follows the rules all the time."

Holy fucking shit. I was kind of joking before, but are Emily and Fiona *actually* going to a sex party? Fucking... fuck. Fuck! Shit. Holy fucking shit, I can't even deal with this.

No. It's fine. Take a deep breath. Breathe, Grey. Do some fucking *namaste* yoga shit right now. There's a reason you go to yoga, right? I mean, the real reason is Emily wanted to go and she was kind of shy and didn't want to go alone, so I just fucking went with her, and then Fiona wanted to go so I was like, yeah, I'll let you two do your thing together, and then they whined and dragged me back into it. And now Fiona wants to keep going, but she wants to go with me, so...

Yoga's cool but I didn't really have a choice in the matter is what I'm saying here.

Anyways, Snapchat. Let's look at this. Defuse my fears, settle my nerves, shove my heart back into my chest before it skydives into a volcano.

The picture pops up. It's a girl in a white dress with a white mask that has a feather sticking out of the top of one side. I don't know what the fuck those shoes are, but they're the kind that make all men stupid. I'm basically an idiot right now, or I was almost a complete idiot, except I looked at the rest of the picture first.

The girl has her hands on her hips with one knee angled in to do a cute and sassy sexy pose, complete with her tongue sticking out.

I know that tongue. I have seen that tongue many times. I have intimate knowledge of that tongue, especially because I've seen it licking up and down my shaft more times than I care to admit. Because, you know, I'm a depraved fucking pervert and I'm having sex with a girl twelve years younger than me.

Going to Hell. Got it. I don't even fucking care. We've gone over this plenty of times and I don't want to deal with it anymore.

But yeah, what the hell? Fiona, why? And where the fuck is Emily?

Oh, there she is. As if seeing Fiona look like the epitome of sex on legs wasn't bad enough, once her picture fades from Snapchat, my sister's pops up. Yeah, uh, I don't want to see that. She's wearing the inverse of Fiona, her dress a steamy red and her shoes pure white.

My sister seriously has to put some clothes on or something. Fiona does too, at least in public. Come to me wearing that in private and I'll gladly fuck the shit out of you, baby girl. Just, uh... at some frat party?

No. No fucking way in Hell.

"Did that get you riled up, handsome?" Holly asks, trying to wind her way to my crotch.

Her fingers tease down my arm while I hold my phone to look at Snapchat, then she slides lower, to my hip, and she tries to sneak her way towards the front of my pants...

13

FIONA

I have a coat, Daddy! I promise I'm still a good girl! That's how I'm going to rationalize this.

I mean, it's February, and it's kind of cold, and Emily and I are wearing dresses that could never ever possibly be called warm, so we have coats. We have them while we wait in line to get into the frat house, at least. I don't even understand the point of a line, because we have masks and everyone in the line has masks, so they should just let us in, right?

But, nope, we need to wait, so we do. And my legs are freezing. Coats are good for a lot of things, but they aren't good for keeping your legs warm.

"We should have worn leggings," I say, my teeth chattering.

"Gertrude!" Emily says, calling me by the dumb name she made up since we're not supposed to tell anyone our real names at this party. "Leggings would ruin our outfits.

I guess we could have put on pantyhose or stockings, but I didn't really think about it."

"This is probably why we never wear dresses," I tell her. "Why are dresses so complicated? You know what I like? Pajama pants and sweatshirts. Really big and fluffy ones."

"You can't wear pajama pants and a sweatshirt to a single's party on Valentine's Day," Emily says, as if she knows all about what you're supposed to do on Valentine's Day at a single's party.

But, nope, she definitely doesn't! I know that for a fact! You've never been to a Valentine's Day single's party either, Emily!

"Why?" I ask, trying to get her to admit she has no idea.

"Because that's not how you get a boyfriend," she says.

I know how to get a boyfriend, Emily. I mean, I wore yoga pants for that one, but pajama pants are kind of like loose yoga pants? I would wear pajama pants to yoga, at least. Just maybe not bikram yoga where they keep the room really hot, because that would be way too hot and sweaty. I only like getting that hot and sweaty when I'm with Daddy, and usually we aren't doing yoga then...

We aren't usually wearing pants, either.

Usually. I'll leave that one up to the imagination...

I can't tell Emily any of this, though. Ugh.

"What if I don't want a boyfriend?" I ask her.

"What do you mean you don't want a boyfriend?" she counters. "I bet there's some nice guys like Daddy here. You should talk to them."

"What wait why?" I stammer. "Um."

"He's nice, you know?" Emily says with a shrug. "I mean, he's my brother, so if I dated a guy like him, that'd be kind of weird, but you could do it and it'd be fine."

"Ha!" I say, sort of laughing? "Ha... ha... you're so funny... I can't date Daddy..."

"I guess technically you could?" Emily says, considering it. She purses her lips and quirks them to one side, making a funny face. "Then we'd be like real sisters, huh?"

"Only if Daddy and I got married," I tell her.

And, oh my gosh, Daddy? Will you marry me? That would be so great. It's a little early and I know that maybe we should take our time, but I'll totally marry the heck out of you. Forever, even.

I don't tell Emily that one, either. I also don't tell Daddy. I don't think I can tell Daddy anything yet. I have my phone and I could text him, but I'm scared.

"Yeah, I don't know if you two could get married," Emily says, nodding a couple times.

"What? Why not?" I ask, sounding far more offended than I mean to.

"Well, he works a lot, you know?" Emily says, nodding again. "And you're way too cute for him."

"Daddy's cute," I counter, mumbling. Daddy's cute, Emily! And handsome and sexy and nice and caring and basically he's the best, so...

"Ooooooohhhhh," Emily says, laughing. "You've got a crush! I've seen the way you look at him. Don't even lie."

"I do not!" I say, my cheeks burning as red as her dress.

She's wearing a coat so thankfully no one can compare the two right now, though.

"Do too."

"Nope."

"Yup!"

"Ladies, ladies, ladies," a guy at the frat house door says, smirking at both of us. "There's more than enough Sigma Epsilon Chi brothers to go around. I'm sure I could find at least three for each of you right now if you're into that kind of thing."

"What kind of thing?" Emily asks, oblivious.

Seriously, Emily? Even I know what he's talking about. Wow.

"Um, no thanks," I say, shaking my head. "I'm just here for the candy."

"We've got plenty of things you can lick and suck on inside," the frat boy says with a wink.

"Whoa, how did you know there was going to be candy?" Emily asks, still oblivious.

"Alice, it's Valentine's Day," I say, deadpan. "Really now!"

"Oh, is that an infraction I hear?" the guy asks, grinning.

"Nope!" Emily says, way more excited about this than I think she ought to be. "We made up fake names to call each other."

"I'm Gertrude tonight, I guess," I say, rolling my eyes.

"The name isn't sexy, but I'm sure you more than make up for it in every other way," he says. "I'll be one of your hosts for tonight. You can call me Seventy-Six. All of my frat brothers are going by numbers, which you can use to find us after the party if we catch your interest. We'll be leaving clues all next week about our true identities. Like a scavenger hunt, but one that ends in love and passion."

Yeah, no. No thank you! Also I just think that's dumb.

You know what nickname I like? Daddy. That's the best one, and it's only for one person, and I'm already in love with him, thank you very much.

"Now if you'll step inside," Seventy-Six says. "Nine-Two will gladly take your coats for you."

"Um, what if I want to keep my coat?" I ask, clinging to it.

"No can do," he says. "Rules are rules. Let's see what you two girls've got. Or should I ask if any of my frat brothers want to frisk you instead? You both look like you could be extra frisky."

"Nope, not today," I say, reluctantly unzipping my fluffy and warm coat.

Seventy-Six or whatever his name is opens the door for us and lets us inside. "Good thing it's night time, Gertrude," he says with a wink.

Ugh!

That was kind of a good line, though. I'm not going to fall for it, but it was kind of good. I'm gonna steal it and use it on Daddy sometime.

GREY

"Oh my fucking God, that's my sister!" I yell, staring at my phone.

Because, first off, it's true. That was Emily, and what the fuck is she doing? Put some damn clothes on, girl. Holy shit.

Second, I figure the easiest way to completely ruin the mood and get Holly to stop trying to ride my cock and grope me on the street is to shout something about my sister. This isn't my proudest moment. I could just tell her to fuck off, but I feel like she's the kind of girl that would like that. Take it as a challenge or something, like... you want to fuck me off, Grey? Aw yeah, let's do it, handsome.

Nah, we're not doing that.

"Well, hopefully she's not the good girl gone wild type," Holly says, trying to salvage this to her advantage. "I'm sure she's fine. Girls just want to have fun, right?"

Nope. No fucking way am I letting you use Cyndi Lauper songs against me, woman.

"Yeah, I've got to go," I say, like this is some serious and immediate issue. It kind of is, so I don't even have to try that hard to make it into one. I take Emily and Fiona very seriously. "Going to drag her ass out of there and..."

I mean, parents spank their kids, but I'm not going to spank Emily. Probably will spank Fiona, though. That's different. She promised me she'd be a good girl--the fucking goodest--and now here she is heading to some sex party whatever the fuck wearing red "fuck me" shoes and a white dress that does nothing to hide any of her curves. If anything, it creates more curves, and let me tell you, Fiona has plenty of fucking curves. Curves for days, all the fucking curves, sexy as hell, ones I want to trace with my tongue for hours on end.

Alright, calm down, Grey. Calm the fuck down. Go... go do something. Where the fuck is the frat house?

And, you know, Holly's right here and she probably knows, so let's just ask her why don't we?

"Where the fuck is the frat house?" I ask. "Which way do I go from here?"

She laughs like I'm joking, then stops when she realizes I'm not. "You can't get in," she says. "They'll have someone at the door. You'll need a mask and a costume to get through. The mask is the ticket, that's what everyone there paid for in order to get in, but if they don't like your costume they'll refuse entry, too."

"Well, I'll get a mask," I say.

"It's just a party, Grey," Holly says, trying to lure me over to her dark side. "Come on, let your sister have a night out and your daughter is probably fine with her, too.

Let's go back to your room, fill up the whirlpool tub, grab a bottle of champagne, and see what happens?"

Yeah, no. You know who I'm going to fill that hot tub up for? Not this chick. Possibly Fiona, but I'm not sure anymore. If she can still walk after I'm done with her, maybe. Or else I guess I could carry her to the tub. That works, too.

I love you, Fiona, and usually you're good. Sometimes not so good, and it's cool. I get it. We don't have to go overboard here, but...

Yeah, tonight is not a good night for anyone.

Where the fuck do I get a mask and a costume from?

15

FIONA

Emily hands her coat over to the frat boy manning the impromptu coat room. It's not even a room so much as a bunch of clothes racks on wheels. He takes one of the hangers and slips off a plastic tile with a number before fitting her coat onto the hanger and hanging it up. Emily takes the plastic tile with her coat number and then it's my turn, I guess.

I reluctantly take off my coat and hand it over to the boy who's apparently going by "Nine-Two" for tonight. Once he hangs up my coat and hands me my numbered tile, he takes a step back and admires me and Emily.

She laughs, nervous, and does a little spin. "What do you think?" she asks him. "Too much."

"Nah," he says with a grin. "Not nearly enough. You're both smoking hot. We don't usually do this, but--"

He trails off and glances from Emily to me then back again.

"What?" she asks, worried.

I'm not worried so much as I feel incredibly under-dressed at the moment. Why did I let Emily convince me this was a good idea? It's not the party so much as the dress, the shoes, and... I mean, that's it. It's the dress and the shoes. I'm glad I have a mask on, at least.

"How would you two fine as hell ladies like to use the *special* entrance?" he asks, gesturing to the hallway behind him.

"The special entrance?" I ask, lifting one brow.

"Mhm," he says, taking a second to rake his eyes up and down my body. Ugh! "You see, we keep the special entrance for VIP guests. From what I can tell, you two fit that perfectly. What are you, juniors, seniors?"

"Um, I'm just a freshman," Emily says, suddenly shy despite being completely gungho about everything two seconds earlier. Really now, Emily! "Is... is that alright?"

"Freshman!" Nine-Two says, smirking at her. "Nah, I never would have guessed. That's actually more than alright. It's great, in fact. Means you'll get to be a VIP around here for a long time. How about you, gorgeous?" he asks, turning to me.

Emily throws me a quick look, which I take to me I should probably lie or tell him I go to school here and I'm a freshman or... I don't know? I don't think she wants me to admit I don't go to their college, though.

"Um, yup!" I say, looking towards my feet. "I'm a freshman too, so..."

Emily lets out a sigh of relief, but Nine-Two doesn't seem to notice.

"Great," he says. "Good stuff. So how about it? You ladies want to use the VIP entrance?"

"It's that way?" Emily asks, looking at the hallway behind him.

"That it is," he says with a nod. "Or you can go down the other hallway. That's the normal one."

"The normal hallway?" I ask, turning around to glance down it.

And... going to be honest, they both look the same. They're on opposite sides of the entrance room, but that's about the only difference. They both have that sort of old, rustic look that I think a lot of frat houses have. Not that I've been in, um... well, this is the first one I've been in. But I've seen movies!

I don't know. I like Daddy's house better. It's not really old, and it doesn't have any crazy architecture or anything, but it's nice and I don't have to worry about VIP hallways or whatever the heck's going on here.

It's a hallway. I don't care. I don't even want to be a VIP, to be honest. I want to go down the regular hallway, but Emily's staring at the VIP hallway like it's the gates to paradise or something and I'm pretty sure I'm going to have to go with her because she's my best friend and that's just what best friends do.

"What about that door?" I ask, pointing over to the closed double doors that are right there, basically just inside the frat house from where we came in, halfway between the hallways on either side of it.

"Yeah, that, no," Nine-Two says, shaking his head. "That's the main room. We're keeping the doors to the common room closed for this party. You've got to choose either the VIP hallway or the regular hallway. Most people don't even get a choice, so you should count yourselves lucky."

"What do you think?" Emily asks me, but she hasn't looked at the regular hallway more than once. She's been staring at the VIP one this entire time, so... Ugh!

"I guess we can go down the VIP hallway if you really want to," I tell her, hesitant.

"Yes!" Emily says, jumping up and down. "This is awesome!"

Nine-Two allows himself an appreciative, extended glance at her breasts as she bounces, but she doesn't seem to notice. I clear my throat and glare at him.

He pulls his eyes away and grins, then stares down at my chest. "Jealous?" he asks. "Don't worry. I'll give you plenty of attention, too."

"Um, no thanks," I say, holding up my hand like a stop sign at a frat boy crosswalk.

I feel like I'm going to end up doing that a lot tonight. I turn to Emily and grab her hand to stop her from putting on more of a show. She looks at me, giddy at first, and then tries her best to calm down.

"Are you ready?" I ask her.

"Ready, Gertrude!" she says.

"Real name?" Nine-Two asks. "That's a--"

"Nope, fake," I say, spinning away from him. I'm done with this. Goodbye!

Emily and I walk towards this supposed VIP hallway. I

don't turn around, but I'm pretty sure the frat boy stares at our butts the whole time. I... I don't like that. I want Daddy to stare at my butt, but I don't like other people doing it. It's weird.

I don't even know why Daddy thought I should spend time with boys my age. They're all pretty dumb from what I can tell. They're nothing like Daddy, and they're definitely not very subtle. I like how Daddy wants me so much, but he tries to hide it a lot. I like how he gets uncontrollably aroused when I'm nearby, but then he'll just pretend like he's not and he'll do something completely different.

Like when we wash the dishes together after dinner? He washes in the sink and I dry them, and he'll act like nothing's wrong, but then when I look down I can see the telltale signs of his throbbing cock pressing hard at the front of his pants. What's that, Daddy? Is that for me? Is it dessert time already? Mmmm...

The fun parts are when he denies it, or he won't give me his cock right away. Sometimes I have to work for it or I have to be a very good girl or...

There's a lot. And it's not just about sex. Sometimes Daddy tells me he has to do work first and then he wants us to sit on the couch and watch a movie, and then... maybe...

I'm a good girl, Daddy. Promise...

None of these guys are like that. They'd probably gladly try to have sex with me immediately, finish in thirty seconds, and then not even care anymore. I don't really know how anyone could enjoy that. Maybe I'm spoiled, though. Probably that's it. I'm basically Daddy's Little Angel, so, um... yup!

Emily and I pass a bunch of doorways on our walk, but they're all closed. We get to the end of this part of the hallway. The only way we can go from here is to take a right and continue down this side of the hallway, so we do that, but I'm starting to have a weird, sinking feeling in the pit of my stomach.

"Emily?" I ask. "It's, um... can we go back and take the regular hallway? I don't like this."

"What?" she asks, giving me a weird look. "It's fine, Fiona. Don't worry. I bet we're almost there."

I know it's *technically* fine. I can hear music coming from the common room on the other side of the wall next to us. The hallway is dim and dark, though. It doesn't look like we belong here, like maybe this part of the frat house is shut off for some reason. And, so, going to be completely honest, but I'm not really a big fan of that? Why would we be going to a closed off part?

We came here to go to a party with a bunch of other people, not to--

The door right next to us swings open suddenly and we stare into the room, blinking through the light. I can't see anything, having gone from having barely any light to way more than enough in a span of half a second. Two guys take our arms, one for me and one for Emily, and they lead us into the overbright room.

I blink and blink again, finally able to see, and, um... what?

We're standing on a stage, with the rest of the large

common area below us, and a horde of people staring up at us. I seriously have no idea what's going on right now.

"Are you ready!" the guy next to Emily shouts into the crowd.

Everyone roars and cheers. Apparently that's for us?

Um... nope, I'm not ready...

GREY

So, look, I don't do this often and I'm not about to make a habit of it, but I feel like if you tell someone you barely know that you're going to rampage through a frat house and drag your sister, who is dressed in something way too fucking provocative, out of said frat house, uh... I mean, seriously, who the fuck goes along with that?

I'm the one doing it and I don't even think I should go along with it. Except, you know, it's Emily and Fiona, so yeah, they're getting their asses dragged out of there. Fiona's getting her ass spanked, too. And a whole bunch of other shit. I don't even fucking know yet, but I'm not happy with the way tonight's going.

Oh, and Holly's still here. I think I kind of made that obvious earlier, but just in case you wanted to know, here's how that went down.

"I'm going to get in that fucking frat house and drag my sister's ass out of there," I told her, and I tried to sound and look a little crazy. No clue if I succeeded, but that was the plan, you know?

"You are?" Holly asked me, biting her bottom lip in thought.

"Yeah, I am," I said. "So you should probably just--"

"Alright, I'll go. Should be fun."

And that's where we're at right now. Me and Holly scoping out the frat house, which is definitely guarded in the front. But seriously, let's be real fucking honest for a second, I can take this kid. It's just one college kid standing at the door and a short line of other college kids waiting to get in. I'm not going to make a habit of beating up college kids or anything, but...

"So what's the plan, sexy?" Holly asks me.

"Can you please stop with the flirting?" I ask her.

"Why? Is it getting to you? You about to give in and let me rock your world back at the hotel?"

"Yeah, not really."

"Damn."

Also I have no plan. Fuck my life. Uh...

The line's a line, and I guess we could go wait in it but we don't have masks. I couldn't care less if Holly has a mask, but I don't have a mask, so doing this legitimately isn't an option at the moment. Kicking a college kid's ass is probably a bad idea, because there's a line full of witnesses. Plus Holly's here and while I wish she'd stop trying to get me to sleep with her, I also don't want to get her fired from her job. So let's cool it on the Rambo shit, I guess is what I'm saying.

I'm not happy about that, but it is what it is.

Since storming into the house isn't exactly a prime option right now, I decide to consider my alternatives. No fucking clue what other choices I have, but that's why it's a good idea to consider them, right? I look around the outside of the house, down the block at some college students standing in a group, then back the way we came, and...

Oh, hey! I've got an idea. Fuck yeah.

"Let's go," I say, because I feel like Holly's my sidekick right now or something and I should probably figure out some badass lines to say. Like a cowboy. Ride off into the fucking sunset and everything.

Holly follows along after me, her heels clicking against the sidewalk. She completely destroys the element of surprise with that one. Also I don't know if these kids have ever seen an attractive woman before, because they all gape at her as we approach.

"Hey," I say to them. "What's up?"

"Uh, hey," one of the guys says. "We don't have any money. Sorry. I'm not really into that kind of thing, either."

I stare at him like he's an idiot, because seriously what the fuck is he talking about?

"What?" I ask.

"You're a pimp, right?" he adds, hesitant. "She's..."

Holly does her own thing, hands on her hips, staring hard at him. "Do I look like a prostitute to you?" she asks.

"Well, you're way too attractive to be hanging out at a frat party," another one of the guys in the group say.

"It's the shoes," the last one adds. "They're a dead giveaway."

"Hey, fuck you," she says, glaring at him. "These were expensive! I'm not a prostitute, but I'd have to be a high class one to afford something like this, and I sure as hell wouldn't be trying to sell myself to broke ass college kids if that was the case."

All three of them shrug, as if, uh... yeah, makes sense? I'm glad we're all agreed that Holly's not a prostitute, because what the fuck does that even have to do with anything? Please disregard the fact that I also thought she was a prostitute when I first talked to her. Look, that's not important right now. What is important is...

"You guys trying to get into the party?" I ask.

"Ugh, yeah," the first kid says. "They wouldn't sell us masks, though. We're not really part of the cool crowd and we're just freshman, so..."

"What are your names?"

"Me? I'm Porter," the first one says.

"Wyatt," the second adds.

"My name's Holden," says the last one.

"Cool. Nice to meet you guys. I'm Grey," I say, holding out my hand and shaking with each of them. We've got some real gentlemanly bonding going on right now. "Oh yeah, and this is Holly, I guess."

"You're an asshole," she says, but then she holds out her hand to shake with all of them so me being an asshole doesn't really change much, now does it?

Also they shake her hand like they aren't sure what to do with it. Guys, holy fuck, stop. She's just a woman that happens to be kind of attractive. That's it. Who the fuck cares?

Anyways...

"So, what's the plan?" I ask them.

"What plan?" Porter counters.

"To get into the party?"

"Uh... you want to get into the party?" Wyatt asks, giving me a weird look.

"Is this some kind of creepy old guy thing?" Holden adds. "Because, uh, yeah... kind of creepy, man."

"Dude..." I say.

"His sister's in there," Holly clarifies.

"Is she hot?" Wyatt immediately asks.

Holden can't keep his mouth shut, either. "Is she single?"

Holly scrunches up her nose and thinks about it. "Yeah, she's pretty cute. I think she's single?"

"Guys!" Porter says, shaking his head at his friends. "He's looking for his sister. This is her fucking brother. How would you like it if someone asked you if your sister was hot and single? Seriously..."

I like this kid. The other ones? Not so much. Porter, though... yeah, seems like a decent guy.

"My sister's twelve," Wyatt says, kind of confused.

"I don't have a sister," Holden adds. "What about my cousin? Everyone says she's hot, but she's just my cousin so no one asks me about her, plus she's married."

"Yeah, uh, can we stop?" I ask them. "I'm here to get into the party. You three want to get in too, right? What's your plan so far?"

"We... we were thinking of trying to bribe the guy at the door," Porter says.

"With what? How much do you have?"

"Fifteen bucks and a stick of gum," Wyatt says, like he's some hardened gumshoe detective. Pretty fucking sure that's where he got the gum from, too.

"Yeah, that's not going to work," I tell them.

"We sort of figured that one out already," Holden says, sighing.

"We can't get masks, right?" I ask.

"They have them right inside," Porter tells me. "There's plenty. They've been giving them to girls who show up who didn't even pay for tickets. What kind of charity event is this?"

"I hate to be the one to tell you this, kid, but it's just a frat party. Yeah, sure they'll give the money to charity but hot girls probably take precedence over optimal donation collection methods."

"Like your sister," Wyatt adds with a knowing nod.

I stare at him and he jumps back like I'm about to smack him. Good call, because I was just about to smack him.

"His daughter, too," Holly says with a grin. "She's in there. They're both dressed to kill."

"Like ninjas?" Holden asks, completely serious.

"Guys!" Porter shouts. "Stop! Fuck!"

Like I said before, I like this kid. He's got potential. I see something in him.

Also, the ninja idea isn't so bad. It's giving me ideas.

What are ninjas good at? Sneaking around. And what do you need in order to sneak around?

Well...

"Alright," I tell them. "I have a plan. Here's what we're going to do..."

GREY

H olly lifts one eyebrow and stares at me. "I'm not sleeping with some college kid."

"What the hell?" I say. "I didn't say you were going to sleep with him. That's not the plan. Stick with the plan and this'll be easier than easy."

"Like me, if I sleep with some college kid," she grumbles.

"You can sleep with me if you want?" Wyatt offers, tossing her a shrug.

Porter and Holden slap him upside the head so I don't have to. It's pretty satisfying to watch. I think we're all working out real well, actually. This plan has merit. I can't say this is my dream team for plans or anything, but we've got some good teamwork going on.

Except, you know, Holly being bitchy about her part in all of this. Look, woman, I didn't ask you to come with me. I didn't even want you here. You volunteered so that's on you. And it's not like we have a lot of time, so we've got to get the ball rolling. Time is of the essence. I've got to get in there, find Fiona and Emily, drag their asses out here, and...

No fucking clue after that. Maybe just drag them all the way back to the hotel, I guess. One over each shoulder should do it. I'm strong, they're small, so it'll work. Or I can look for a wheelbarrow or something and toss them in then push them back. I don't know why I'm thinking up methods to drag them back, because for all I know maybe they'll see the error of their ways and gladly walk back with me. All fucking pouty, too.

I can see it now. Fiona's just being super fucking pouty, bottom lip pushed out as she looks at me under her lashes, batting her eyes every so often. Sorry, Daddy...

And then Emily being a grumpy fuck like she's mad at me because I'm right and I'm smarter than her when it comes to this shit. Look, Emily, I'm a guy. I know guys. Yeah, you're my sister, and I understand that you're a girl, you don't know guys. Have you even fucking dated a guy? No. How do I know? Well, that's a secret, and I'm sure as fuck not going to tell her that Fiona tells me every-thing. I need my sexy little spy to keep it up so I don't have to worry about my little sister.

So that's how this is going to go. Deal with it, brat.

"Alright, looks like the line is gone," I say to Holly, ignoring everything she was just trying to say to me.

Look, I'm not throwing her to the wolves. She's a grown ass woman and I'm right the fuck here. The frat bro standing at the front door is like... a hundred fifty pounds soaking wet and shorter than Holly even when she doesn't have heels on, which she does, so basically she's towering over him and no one has anything to worry about.

"This is bullshit," she says, but she saunters off towards the door anyways. Yeah, there we go...

"I don't think this is going to work," Holden says, watching her go.

"Look at that ass," Wyatt says without a care in the world.

"We're getting into the party," Porter says, determined.

I seriously have no idea why these guys even want to go to this party. I mean, I can see why Wyatt wants to go. Holden might be some of the same. Porter seems like a good kid, though. Go find a nice girl to date, dude. Have fun with her, ignore this stupid party bullshit.

It seems fun, but it comes at a cost, you know? You wake up the next day with a roaring headache, and maybe you had fun the night before, but you're not going to do anything the day after and who the fuck wants that? You lost a day of potential fun because you wanted to trade it for a couple hours of... I don't even fucking know. Vaguely swaying side to side, pretending to dance, with music so loud that you can't hear anything anyone's saying?

Dancing's cool. Go fucking dance. Go to a club and dance your ass off. Drink a lot of fucking water, lay off the booze for the time being unless you want a few glasses of whatever the fuck to ease the tension and let loose, and then have a great time.

Girls like that a lot more than drunken idiots who only want to sleep with them.

I think they do, at least. I'm not a girl, so who the fuck

knows? Just saying, I think they'd be more appreciative of the fun and dancing than the drunken idiocy. Not that girls are immune to drunken idiocy, either.

Fuck, I don't want Emily to turn twenty-one. That's going to suck balls. And she better not even fucking think about sucking balls. That's my little sister, you asshole! Keep your balls to yourself. Holy shit.

"What's she saying?" Holden asks as we watch Holly from our vantage point down the street.

"She's following the plan," I tell him. "Don't even worry about it."

"I'm not worried, but... where's she going to go after this?"

"Inside, probably," I say with a shrug.

"What if he locks the door behind them?" Porter asks.

Uh... fuck. Fucking...

I didn't even think about that? I came up with this plan on the spot, alright? Sorry I didn't have time to make it foolproof.

"Do any of you know how to pick locks?" I ask, casual, like these kids must do that all the time.

"Nope," Holden says.

"Not really," Porter adds.

"Actually..." Wyatt says with a grin.

Yeah, how did I guess that one? This kid. What a pervert. It's cool, though. We can bring him over to the good side. This'll be my Jedi redemption story or some-thing. Not today, Darth Wyatt.

Holly finishes up with her flirtations. No clue why it

took so long. Just fucking jiggle your boobs, woman. It's a college dude in a frat. This shouldn't be that hard.

He takes her hand and she bristles, but he doesn't seem to notice. As they saunter into the house, this frat bro looking like he won a free pass to a candy store buffet, she turns to look at us. She gives us a thumbs up, followed by an "okay" sign, and then a wink, and all the other fucking "all good" things she can think of. Thankfully the frat dude doesn't notice, or doesn't care. No clue which.

"Mua ha ha!" Wyatt says, pulling out a pair of lockpick tools from who the fuck knows where. Why, dude? Why?

"Wyatt, can you cool it with the evil maniacal laughter?" I ask him.

"Sorry," he says. "How about this? Mua--"

That's it. He stops at the first one.

"Yeah, that's not really working for me, either."

"How about we get in this party?" Porter asks. "We've been standing outside for two hours and it's getting kind of cold."

You can say a lot about these guys. We've got a pervert who can pick locks, another pervert who is slightly less obvious about it, and then good guy Porter who should probably just find a nice girl to go dancing with. I feel like there's a lot wrong with them, but the one thing they do well is they're dedication towards a common cause.

This is it. This is my A Team. We've got this, guys. Roll out!

We swagger towards the frat house like we own the place. So fucking badass, let me tell you.

It's probably not badass, but let's just go with it. I think

Wyatt ran into a bush on accident, but it's dark out and the streetlights here are scarce. Just... no. Don't focus on that.

Focus on how badass we are. Look at this fucking swagger. Confidence! Fuck yeah!

We get to the door, ready to break our way in. Wyatt strides confidently forward, the tools of his perverted trade in hand, prepared for anything. I stand guard, ready to do my thing, and Porter and Holden keep an eye out at the steps in case anyone tries to flank us.

Then Wyatt turns the knob and the door opens. "Oh, it's unlocked," he says. "Cool."

Fuck this. We swaggered over here and for what? Bull-shit, that's what this is. Complete and utter bullshit.

"Now what?" I ask.

"Uh, we should be able to get masks in the--"

"My dudes," somebody says from inside. "You coming in or what? Did you see that hot piece of tail Dylan just brought in? Fucking A!"

"Who the fuck is that?" I ask, hushed.

"Sounds like Brad," Porter says with a shrug.

"Who the fuck is Brad?"

"Hey, Brad," Porter says. "We forgot our masks. Is it cool if--"

"Yeah, yeah. I got you," Brad says as we step inside. "Sorry about Dylan. He's a dick sometimes. I would have just given you masks but the whole frat brotherhood thing, you know? Don't tell him I let you in, alright?"

"Sure," Porter says with the most 'nice guy' smile I've ever seen. "Thanks a lot. Are we still on for studying next week?"

"Man, that would be so fucking helpful. I'd really appreciate it. It's like... you'd think people here would study more. I thought frats were about helping each other. But everyone's kind of shit at it, and getting C's is cool for some people, but my parents freak out and I just don't want to deal with that."

"It's cool," Porter says. "No problem, man."

"Thanks, dude," Brad says, then looks at me. "Who's this?"

"Grey," Porter says, introducing me. "Grey, this is Brad."

"Nice to meet you, man," Brad says with a frat bro nod. "You guys can borrow some shit from my room if you want. Should probably dress up or something. If you hurry, the last auction's about to start. Should be cool."

"Auction?" I ask.

"Yeah. These girls came in earlier. Red and white outfits. Matching, but opposites or whatever. Angel and demon? I don't know. But since this is a single's party, part of what we're doing is a fun auction thing for charity. It's all for a good cause. It's actually--"

I don't hear the rest, because, uh... yeah... auction? My sister is being sold off. Fiona, too. Sold off for what? A fucking single's thing for charity? What the hell does that mean?

Who even cares what it means? I don't like it, even if I have no idea what the fuck it is. I don't have to know to know that I hate it.

And it's starting soon. Fuck.

I grab my mask, shove it over my face like Zorro or something, and head out. To somewhere.

"Uh...?" I ask, looking left and right down two completely separate hallways.

"That way," Brad says, pointing right. "Room 105 halfway down the hall. See you guys later."

I think we have a little more than swagger this time. We're professionals walking with our backs to a massive explosion, action-packed movie hero style. There's no actual explosion yet, though. Kind of tempted to just blow up this frat house, to be honest. I'm not going to, but I'm kind of tempted.

Emily's grounded by the way. For life. She's never leaving the house again.

I'll figure out Fiona's punishment after that. Sorry, but it's not going to be good, baby girl. You might never be able to sit again. Or I'll just tie her to my bed, maybe put a leash on her, some kind of fucking... GPS tracking device? I don't know.

I'll deal with it later. Soon.

FIONA

I don't know what the heck kind of party Emily brought me to, but this is just some weird stuff that's going on. I don't like it! Also, I want Daddy to be here. I'd like it then. But Daddy's not here, and I don't know how he could even get in here, so that's kind of out of the question.

Ugh. Ugh ugh ugh!

I know I'm supposed to be an adult now that I'm eighteen but I don't want to be that right now. I don't know what I want to be instead, but I want to whine and pout and... and do a lot of other stuff like that.

I'm a good girl for Daddy and Daddy only. I don't have to be a good girl for these people.

I mean, I probably shouldn't throw a tantrum in front of Emily. That could be embarrassing. I don't even know anyone else in here and I'm wearing a mask, so from what I can see it doesn't matter what I do. Except then there's Emily standing right next to me, so...

"Um, Fiona?" she whispers, looking at me sideways.

"Yes, Alice?" I answer, emphasizing her fake name.

"Oh, shoot!" she says, glancing around quick to make sure no one heard her. No one did, so we're good for now. "Sorry, um, Gertrude..."

As soon as she says my fake name, she bursts into a giggle fit. The crowd of college students in front of us starts to cheer, as if this is some planned addition and it's for their benefit. No, it's not! Emily's giggling because we're stupid eighteen year old girls doing stupid silly stuff like coming up with stupid names for this stupid party. I'm not going to admit any of that out loud, I really don't want to admit we're being dumb, but it is what it is, you know?

"Are you girls ready?" the announcer next to us on stage asks.

"Um, no?" I say, raising one eyebrow at him. Do you think that'll work?

"It's for charity," he adds with a grin.

"It *is* for charity, Gertrude," Emily says. "That makes it good, right?"

Emily, no. No no no. Emily Emily Emily...

So basically this is what's going on, just so you know. Before this, the frat boy up here with us spelled out all the rules.

These are those:

- **a)** All proceeds go to charity. Yeah!

- **b)** Bidding will start at twenty dollars and continue until one person is the definite winner.

Bidding wars may go on indefinitely. For charity. Yeah!

- **c)** What's everyone bidding on? Us, apparently. Me and Emily. Separately, though. The winner gets to take the girl he won into the secret mystery room for seven minutes.

- **d)** Seven minutes. In heaven. That's what this is. You know that game? You go into a closet or something with someone and you do whatever for seven minutes. People make out, or they talk, or they have sex, I guess?

I've never had sex in a closet and I'm not about to start. I mean, if Daddy wants to have sex with me in a closet for some reason, I'm alright with that. I feel like a closet is really small, though. Can it be a big walk-in closet? Also, why a closet? I think the bedroom is fine, or basically any other room.

We've had sex in the bathroom before, and that's really fun, but bathrooms are different. Bathrooms have showers. Closets don't have showers. At least I don't think anyone would put a shower in their closet. I bet Daddy would know the answer to that one. He's very smart, and I know it's a dumb question but if I asked him he wouldn't make fun of me. Daddy loves me.

So anyways, supposedly we're being sold off to go into some room that may or may not be a closet. For charity. Yeah!

Nope. Not buying it. I'm worth a lot. Like... I don't know how much. Hold on.

"Alice, how much do you think we're worth?" I ask her.

"Um, more than twenty dollars, I hope," she says.

"Let's start the bidding at twenty dollars. Do I hear twenty?" the frat announcer asks the crowd.

Someone immediately raises their hand.

"Twenty!" the announcer announces, because that's what announcers do. "Twenty-five?"

"Thirty!" someone shouts, raising their hand.

"Thirty! Do I--yes! Thirty-five. Forty. Forty-five!"

"Looks like we're worth at least fifty dollars," I tell Emily, mumbling under my breath.

"Well, that's for you," she says. "Do you think we're worth the same?"

"We're definitely worth at least the same," I say with a nod. "I mean, really close if nothing else. Like maybe I'm fifty and you're fifty-five or something like that."

"That's it, though?" Emily asks. "What do we do when we go in the room?"

I shrug. "I don't know. I wasn't really planning on doing anything."

"What if the guy who buys you wants to kiss you, though? Are you going to do it? It's only for seven minutes."

"What? No! That's--"

I'm not kissing anyone! Nope! No way!

Also I'm up to seventy-five dollars now. I don't know how I feel about this. Daddy has a lot of money because he owns his own business and I'm pretty sure he'd say I'm worth way more than seventy-five dollars. Like... a lot more. I don't know how much more. That's up to Daddy to decide.

I mean, I know the real answer. I'm priceless! But this is a charity auction and I don't think they accept that as an option.

They should, though. I'm still waiting for someone to bid infinity dollars. All of the dollars, please! Yes, for the girl in the white dress and the red shoes and the boobs that are basically spilling out of the white dress, and...

Oh no. I'm on stage, aren't I? I mean, it's not that far up, but people are looking at us, and we're standing above them, and...

I push my knees together all of a sudden, shy and worried that someone might have been able to peek up my dress. The guys standing closest to the stage laugh, and a bunch of girls standing around the room roll their eyes at me.

"Two-hundred!" someone near the back shouts.

"Brother?" the announcer asks, acting like he's surprised. "Are you sure?"

"For that hot little thing? Fuck yeah, man. That's a bargain."

You're damn fucking right it's a bargain, because I'm priceless, but that doesn't mean you get to bid on me, you... you...

"Two-hundred dollars?" Emily asks, staring at me. "Fi... Gertrude! Holy what the heck!"

"I think it's fine to say holy shit or holy fuck," I tell her.

"We're in a frat house. I'm not sure this is like church or going out in public."

"Oh," she says with a nod. "I guess not, but I don't know. I think Daddy would be mad if we started cursing all over the place."

"Probably," I say. And... I'm sorry, Daddy! Not about the cursing. I mean, I'm sorry about that, but...

I don't want to be sold for two-hundred dollars. Or anything. I mean, I guess I'll just go stand in the room and do nothing, but still.

I have to tell Daddy about this, and that's the part I don't like. It's like, yup, I sold myself? It was a charity auction! I didn't have sex. Ugh. I'm not a prostitute, Daddy! And I didn't like doing this. No, I didn't kiss him! I didn't do anything. It was just seven minutes and it was dumb and afterwards I went out and danced with Emily and I didn't even talk to any of the boys there because they aren't my Daddy and I don't like them and...

"Can we do a group bid?" someone asks in the back. "Does she take more than one guy at a time?"

"It's in the rules!" the announcer says, gleeful. "You can all go in the room, but it's up to the girl as far as what she'll do. I will say that most girls are extremely interested, so..."

Nope. Not interested. No thank you.

"Three-hundred," the group of boys who is apparently going to try and go into a room with me says.

"Whoa, that's a new high for the night!" the frat announcer on stage shouts out. "Is this it then? Any more bids?"

"I'm definitely worth a lot more than three-hundred," I say, crossing my arms over my chest.

Which... maybe is a bad idea...?

This tube dress is already causing me some cleavage issues. When I cross my hands over my chest, or more specifically under my breasts, I just kind of prop them up on accident and show them off. Totally not my intent, either!

I'm not... I...

"Three-fifty!" the other guy who bid two-hundred earlier says. "We'll go in as a group, too. Looks like that's what she wants."

Noooooopppppppeeeeee!

I glare, or I try to, and I'm just going to quit now. Everytime I do anything that's supposed to look annoyed or frustrated or completely uninterested, these stupid boys keep bidding higher. It's dumb. They're dumb. I'm probably dumb for being here. Why don't we just go home?

I don't like this. I wish Daddy was here with me. I...

19

GREY

B rad's room is basically a closet. Seriously, I think this must have been a closet way back in the day when they first built this place. I don't know what else you could use a room like this for.

Except, you know, a dorm room, I guess. This is why I don't regret not having the "full college experience" of staying in dorms and dealing with all of the bullshit that entails. Emily's dorm room isn't this small, but she also has to share it with a roommate, so it's not like it's much better, either.

I share my entire house with Fiona, and most of the time she just spends it in the same room as me, but that's nowhere near the same. Fiona's cute and adorable and she likes to lay her head in my lap and watch TV while I'm looking at work documents.

She gets so fucking excited when all my work is done and I give in and lay my head in her lap, too. I don't even fucking know. I never knew I wanted to rest my head in a girl's lap before, but holy shit it's amazing. With Fiona, at least. Maybe not everyone else. I don't really care about everyone else, I only care about her, so yeah.

She'll run her fingers through my hair and play with it while we just sit there, or I lay there I guess, and we watch a movie or something. And then she'll stare down at me like she wants something, so I glance up at her and give her a goofy look. That's her cue to lean down quick and give me a kiss and then giggle uncontrollably like she did something naughty.

Fuck. I love her so much. I can't even fucking--

Enough of that for now, though. I'm trapped in a closet-sized bedroom with three other guys and we're supposed to be finding costumes for this Valentine's Day Singles Party. The Sigma Epsilon Chi plaque hangs on the back side of the door, taunting me.

S.E.X.

Seriously, what bullshit is that? I'm not a fan. No clue why Fiona and Emily couldn't have gone to a regular party. With like... balloons. Balloons and cake and a fucking pinata or something. Real wholesome shit, you know?

"Uh, what do you want?" Wyatt asks Holden.

"I'll take this," he says, grabbing a basketball jersey.

"You want this, Grey?" Porter asks me.

I look at what he's got. He holds out a dark superhero

kind of cape in both hands. Sort of like Batman, except this is thin and black with not much to it. Maybe more like a vampire? I don't know.

"I think it looks pretty cool," Porter adds with a shrug. "Probably the coolest thing here."

"Sure," I say, grinning at him. "Thanks, man."

I take the cape from him while he smiles like he just did something awesome. And he kind of did, not going to lie. Once I wrap the cape around me and tie the straps together by my neck, I feel pretty badass. Maybe not completely like Batman, but pretty fucking close.

Porter puts on a gray vest and Wyatt finds this goofy as fuck hat to wear. We aren't winning any costume contests, but it's better than nothing.

"Alright, can we get out of here?" I say. "You guys are great, but I'm not a huge fan of this whole balls to the wall thing, literally."

"Sometimes you've just got to put your balls to the wall and get it done," Wyatt says with a sigh.

"Do you want me to smack him?" Holden asks.

"Nah, it's cool," I say. "He's growing on me."

"Let's go save your sister, Grey," Porter says, giving me a thumbs up. Sort of rough considering our close proximity but he does his best.

"Let's do it."

We struggle to get the door open, then to get out the door. As we're leaving, Holly passes us in the hall. She smirks at me and winks.

"Nice outfit, Superman," she says, licking her lips.

"It's Batman, dammit!" I say, groaning.

"Whatever. Have fun, boys. I'm out. Slipped away to the bathroom, or that's what I said, and now my work here is done. See you back at the hotel, Grey."

Maybe she's not so bad. I mean, she's pretty bad, and I'm not going to sleep with her, but I appreciate the assist. This whole night is kind of fucking weird, and I'm not sure what the hell is going on anymore, but...

I'm making new friends? That's cool, right? Can't say I ever expected to do that, especially at Emily's college, but I'm Batman now or something so I should probably expect the unexpected. I think that's how it works. That guy plans for everything.

We head down the hall towards the sound of... *something*. No fucking clue. People are roaring out words that barely make sense and some other guy is controlling the crowd with other words that sound like numbers or something.

Oh shit. The auction. Are we too late? Fuck fuck fuck.

"Hurry!" I say, urging my new friends on. "Fucking..."

We rush down the dim hallway and turn at the end. A pair of double doors opens up a little further down, lights from inside spilling out. Me and the guys step through into this huge, open and expansive room. The crowd roars, people shout out, everyone is screaming.

I look to the other side of the room and see Emily and Fiona standing on stage. Emily looks pouty and Fiona is obviously flustered. What the fuck happened? Is it too late?

The guy on stage shouts out, "Five-hundred going once! Five-hundred going twice!"

Shit. Fuck. Shit fuck cock mother asshole bastard fucker...

20
FIONA

Everyone's staring at me like I'm meat and the bidding keeps going up and up. I don't think this is normal. A few of the girls in the crowd look really pissed off at the fact that I'm apparently bringing in some huge, previously unheard of price.

Well, you know what? It's not my fault! I didn't even want to wear this dress, which is honestly way too much. Why is it that all of my wardrobe issues or malfunctions or whatever you want to call them end up involving Emily? That's not entirely true, though. Sometimes they involved Daddy but those ones are a lot more calculated and intentional. Those are the complicated ones and I don't have time to explain that right now.

One, two, three, four. Hundreds of dollars. Twenty-five, fifty, seventy-five. I don't know what's even going on anymore. I'm not sure what I'm going to sell for, and if I'm being incredibly honest I don't want to be sold to any of these guys anyways.

The bidding slows down eventually, but both groups of guys that are still going keep staring at me. It's like they're waiting for me to do something, but I don't know what. Do they think I'm going to start acting like a stripper? Because, um... no. Nope! Not going to happen, boys.

I wouldn't mind stripping for Daddy, though. Privately, I mean. If I just came up to him while he was sitting on the couch and distracted him by swaying my hips side to side, seductive, until he couldn't take his eyes off me. Daddy doesn't look at me like I'm meat, not like some generic fast food burger on his plate when he's hungry and he doesn't care what he eats. Not even like filet mignon, which I used to think was really good, but...

No, Daddy looks at me like I'm the highest quality possible, like I'm some prime cut of Japanese A5 Kobe steak. And I've never had that, so I don't know how good it is, but Daddy assures me it's the best meat that money can buy and it's amazing.

That's me. I'm amazing! Thank you, Daddy...

So honestly it's really frustrating to be looked at like I'm a burger by frat boys who aren't anywhere near as wonderful as Daddy. Maybe it's frustrating to the girls in the audience around the stage, and I can sort of see why they'd be jealous. I used to get jealous when girls would flirt with Daddy, and I still kind of do. Like that woman at the hotel? Ugh!

A new group of guys walks into the main reception room, stepping through the door opposite where Emily and I are standing. I look over quick, just because I see them coming in. Nothing interesting there, no reason to...

Um... hello there...

Wait, no! I didn't just think that. Nope, not even a little, not at all, no way no how, nuh uh...

I don't know, but the tallest guy that just walked in, the one wearing a smooth black cape like he's some sort of suave and sophisticated prince or maybe a superhero (or a supervillain?) or a vampire or... I mean, basically all of the sexiest kinds of guys in stories look like he looks, with his cape and his red mask. His hair is mussed up a little, almost like he woke up that way, except in the best possible way.

Daddy has hair like that sometimes. Did he have hair like that today? I think he might have, which is even more annoying, because why does this sexy guy who just walked in remind me of Daddy? I don't like that. Daddy should remind me of Daddy, not this sexy vampire dark superhero prince.

The four guys who just walked in take a few seconds to survey their surroundings. I don't mean to stare, but there's just something about him... I don't know what, but...

And then I realize the final bid is coming to a close. Oh no. No no no no no!

"Five-hundred going once! Five-hundred going twice!"

Sold. That's what's next. I'm pretty sure that's how this works. We haven't gotten there yet, but I've seen auctions and stuff in movies, so I think I know how this usually goes.

"One-thousand!" someone shouts from the back.

The room grows quiet. No one says anything for the

longest time. The girls glare hard at me, faces red, seething. The guys all turn, dazed and confused, looking towards the voice that just doubled and destroyed their bid in the span of half a second. Even the announcer on stage stands there with his mouth wide open, staring into a void of nothingness in front of him.

It's him. The person who bid on me is the black cape wearing man who just stepped into the room. With his three friends. And, um... what does that mean?

The announcer wants to know, too. "Is that a group bid?" he asks, hopeful, like maybe this is the only way he can make sense of the situation.

"What? No. She's mine," he says, his tone gruff despite the easiness with which he says those words.

I'm his. Take me...

Wait, no, I'm not yours, asshole! I'm Daddy's! And I don't care how sexy you kind of look. It's just the lighting probably. It's not exactly super bright in here. It's a little dark and he's way in the back, and...

"Anyone else?" the announcer asks. "Yeah, not sure how you can top that. Going once. Going twice. And... sold to billionaire Bruce Wayne in the back!"

He's a billionaire? Um, no. I'm dumb. Ugh. Bruce Wayne is Batman. Duh, Fiona...

"Batman, huh?" Emily asks, grinning at me. "I wonder what kind of gadgets he brought?"

"Emi--" I start to say. "*Alice*. Really now. Ugh."

"I'm just saying, Batman has all sorts of gadgets, and I'm sure some of them could be really kinky, right? He could tie you up with the rope from a grappling hook baterang or something."

"Alright, since when are you into Batman?" I ask her, hands on my hips.

"Who *isn't* into Batman?" she asks, confused.

"Um, me," I say. "I'm not."

"You sure? Because that guy in the Batman cape looks like all sorts of your type."

"He's not," I say, stomping one foot. "I'm not going to--"

We're cut off by the guy on stage who wants to start up the next auction. "Next up is the lovely--" he says, turning towards her.

"Alice," she says with a sugary sweet smile.

"Alice! Which is probably not her real name, or else someone's about to get a penalty tonight."

The crowd laughs and Emily just shakes her finger at them and grins. "Nope!"

"We'll start the bidding higher. This is the last auction of the night, everyone. Can we get one-hundred?"

Mr. Sexy Batman in the back is talking to one of his sidekicks or whoever the other guys he's with are. They're arguing about something, but they look more flustered than anything. The boy in the grey vest shakes his head and holds his hands up. Nope. No way. Not going to...

The guy in the cape glares at him, though. Grey Vest balks and looks down for a second. The Caped Avenger pats him on the shoulder and it seems like they have a moment of understanding.

"One-twenty-five! Do I hear one-thirty?"

"A thousand," someone says, loudly muttering, not nearly as confident as the previous four-figure shout.

"Uh, what?" the guy on stage with us asks. "Can you say that again?"

"A thousand!" he shouts.

It's the guy with my sexy superhero bidder. Grey Vest holds his hand up, looking like he's about to pass out or die or everything else nerve-wracking all at once.

"Uh, sure, well..." the announcer says, even more confused the second time around. "Anyone else? Going once. Twice. Sold..."

And that's how Emily and I got sold at a charity auction for seven minutes of action in a back room at a frat house.

Best Valentine's Day ever or what? Yeah, um...

Actually, it didn't turn out so bad...

GREY

"Grey, I can't."

"You have to, Porter. You're the only one who can do this."

"I'd do it," Wyatt says. "Dude, your sister's hot."

Which gets him a slap upside the head from Holden. These guys are good. They're like my apprentices now. I've taken them under my wing, or my cape, or however the fuck this works. I don't know. We're still hammering out the details, but so far so good.

"I really don't think this is a good idea," Porter says.

"It's a great idea," I tell him. "You're the only one I can trust to do this."

"It's your sister, though! I... I can't do it."

"Look, it's not like you're going to have sex with her. You're just making sure that no one else tries."

"What if she tries to have sex with me, though?" he asks, turning his eyes towards the stage.

"She's not going to try and have sex with you," I tell

him, point blank. "No sex is happening. This is a no sex zone."

"You realize this is the Sigma Epsilon Chi frat house?" Holden chimes in. "It's the opposite of a no sex zone."

"Alright, *this* zone," I say, clarifying. I wave my hands around us like I'm creating some invisible bubble. "This is a no sex zone."

"You won't be in the room with us, though," Porter reminds me. "What then?"

"Dude, let's make this simple. Do you want to sleep with my sister? You don't, right? So what's the issue?"

"Is that a serious question?" Porter asks. "Do you want me to tell you the truth or am I supposed to lie?"

"Alright, uh... let's try that again," I say, trying to figure this out. "Out of everyone here, I trust you the most as far as not sleeping with my sister. How's that?"

"Grey, that's the problem," Porter says, struggling. "I'm not going to try, you know? But... so if *she* tries I don't think I'm going to be able to say no. I'm not that strong."

I have the weirdest admiration for him right now. I'm not sure why, because we're talking about sex with my sister, and this is completely off limits. Not happening ever. Emily can have sex when I'm dead. That's plenty of time. More than enough, really.

"Have you had sex before?" I ask him.

He doesn't answer with words, but just shakes his head.

"Alright, Emily hasn't either, so the odds of her going full seductress on you are pretty low, right?"

"I guess so?" he says with a shrug. "I don't know."

"Here's what you do," I tell him. "The odds are low, so in order to lower them even more you have to get her chatting. Emily loves to talk about stuff. Tell her how much you like her shoes, and she'll basically tell you everything about her shoes and how much she likes them, too. Ask her about how she likes college. That kind of shit. Between those two questions, I think you'll easily waste away seven minutes, and then you'll be out of there and you won't have to worry about it."

"What if I tell her that you're here?" he asks. "That'll help, right?"

"Uh, yeah... no. No fucking way. No one is telling Emily I'm here. Out of the question. She'll be pissed. We've salvaged this, and we're going to finish salvaging it, but after that I'm going incognito. As long as no other bullshit pops up, we're just going to hang out here or whatever, do nothing even remotely sexual, and then go home. Alright? That's the deal, guys. I got you into this party and now I need your help keeping everyone in line. Are we good?"

"Good," Porter and Holden say together.

"When you say nothing even remotely sexual, what exactly do you--" Wyatt starts to ask, but then gets a double smack upside the head. "Alright, fine!"

"Glad we're all in agreement," I say with a grin. "You're up then, Porter. Do your thing, my man."

"I... alright, I guess..." he says. And then in the meekest attempt at an auction bid ever, he mumbles loudly. "A thousand."

All eyes are on him. We just went from a hundred-something right to one-thousand. The guy on stage who

141

took it upon himself to auction off my little sister and Fiona stares into the crowd, trying to find the owner of that last bid.

"Uh, what? Can you say that again?" he asks.

"A thousand!" Porter shouts. Yeah, there we go. Much better. Good job.

The auction ends after that. We've won. I'm not exactly happy about paying two grand to get my sister and Fiona out of being sold to the highest bidder. I mean, in this case I'm the highest bidder, but still. I guess it's for charity so that's cool. I'm doing my part for the community?

Fiona's ass is going to pay me back in spades once I'm alone in that room with her. I hope you're ready for this, baby girl...

"The girls are going to get ready while we sort out the payments," Frat Bro Announcer says. "If you guys could head over to the payment booth we'll get this squared away."

Porter and I walk to this table, which is apparently the payment booth. Some people lead Fiona and Emily off the stage, bringing them to the room or rooms or whatever. I really fucking hope this isn't another closet situation like that other frat dude's room we used earlier. I kind of feel like it will be, and I guess I'll deal with it, but...

"Do you have two-thousand dollars on you?" Porter asks me. "I forgot to ask."

"What, in cash?" I ask, looking over at him. "I'm sure they take--"

Shit. I don't have my checkbook on me. Who even writes checks anymore? And yeah, I'm not in the habit of carrying around massive wads of cash, either. Seems like a terrible idea.

"Hey guys," this girl in glasses says behind the payment table. "That's one-thousand each! Thanks so much for your contribution. It's going to a great cause."

"Yeah, uh..." I say, trailing off.

She tilts her head down and stares at me over the rims of her glasses. "You've got the money, right?"

Hey there, Little Miss Money Mafia, calm the fuck down. Seriously though, this girl is scary.

"Look," I tell her. Time to be truthful, Grey. "I do, but I don't carry that much in cash and I don't have any checks on me. Do you take credit cards?"

"Dude, do you see a credit card swiper? That's not how this works."

"Is there an ATM nearby?" I offer.

She sighs like she's already tired of dealing with me even though we've only been talking for thirty seconds.

"Who uses an ATM anymore?" she asks. "That's for my parents. If you don't have the cash on you, you can send it to one of the frat house funding accounts. We have accounts with all of the major cash apps, so whichever one you use is fine."

"My preferred cash app...?" I say, looking over at Porter. What the fuck?

"I use Venmo," he says. "Lots of people use that one. It's really easy."

"Venmo," I tell Miss Mafia.

"Here's the info," she says, sliding me a card.

Porter helps me out and we get Venmo downloaded

onto my phone, hook up my credit card to it, and send way more money than I really want to send over to the Sigma Epsilon Chi frat house charity account. Little Miss Money Mafia accountant over here confirms the payment on her end once we're through and then she nods.

"Nice doing business with you!" she says, chipper. "Enjoy the party, guys."

"Hey, uh... just wondering, but why are you the one managing the auction payments?" I ask.

"Huh?" she says.

"You know... you're a girl, and this is a frat, so..."

"That's kind of old school thinking, isn't it?" she asks.

"I mean, it's a *frat*," I say. That's my point. That's the entire point I'm trying to make.

"So?"

"Yeah, you know what? I don't know," I tell her. "Alright, where do we go?"

"That way," she says, pointing to the far end of the room.

An open door leads to an empty hallway, and a pair of football player looking jock dudes are standing outside, guarding the entrance.

"This is a terrible idea," Porter says. "I just want to go on the record as saying this is a really bad idea."

"It's fine," I say to him. "Calm down. Talk about her shoes. Everything's fine."

22

FIONA

A guy and a girl rush Emily and I off the stage over to a different hallway from the one we came in. This one doesn't seem to be connected to the other one. No one says anything as we walk.

"Um, excuse me?" I ask, to whoever. I don't know who I should be talking to, but I'm really not happy with the situation so far, so...

"Yes?" the girl says, spinning around to look at me.

"Where are we going?"

"The room?" she says, giving me a weird look. "You don't have to do anything, by the way. You can just sit at the other end. That's what some girls do, but sometimes the guys who bid on them try to make it sound like more happened. It's cool if you don't want to do anything, though."

"Oh," I say.

"What if we want to do something?" Emily asks. "Um, I'm asking for a friend."

"What friend?" I ask her.

"You," she says. "I saw the way you were looking at that guy..."

"I was not!"

"Yup, uh huh... sure..."

"I mean, I was looking, because... he just came in the room and bid a thousand dollars. That's the only reason I was looking."

"Right. Uh huh. Sure..."

"Shut up."

The guy and the girl showing us the way to the rooms for our sudden Seven Minutes in Heaven auction laugh.

"We'll be right outside," the guy says. "So if you need anything, just yell. We're not about doing anything non-consensual here, so if one of the guys tries anything you don't like, you can speak up, alright?"

"And if everything's consensual, you might want to keep the noise down," the girl adds. "We need to open the door if anything sounds even remotely suspicious. Dean's rule. The entire frat could get shut down if we don't follow it, so... yup, you probably don't want us walking in just because you two decided to do some headboard breaking or bed shaking or love making or..."

"I won't," I say, firm.

I don't care if the guy was kind of attractive! He's not Daddy, he just sort of reminded me of Daddy, and seriously those are two entirely different things. It's not even close to the same!

"You should get his number," Emily says.

We're there now, standing outside the doors. Do we go

in? Neither the guy nor the girl says anything, they both just stand with us, so apparently not.

"What do I want his number for?" I ask her.

"For the next time you come visit? You two can hang out!"

"Hang out...?" I ask.

"Yeah, you know? Hang out," she says. "With clothes on. Or not. You know how it is?"

I mean, I do know how it is, because Daddy and I *"hang out"* without clothes on, um... kind of a lot? It's not like we do it all the time, but sometimes it's just fun being naked together, and if we don't have to do anything important and we're probably just going to take our clothes off again later, why not?

It's like making the bed. Why make the bed if you're going to get into it again later? Except this is clothes and not wearing them, but I swear it's basically the same thing.

"Ohhhhh, you've got a crush!" Emily says, giggling. "I can see it in your eyes!"

"I do not!" I protest.

"I got the text," the guy says, interrupting us.

"Same," the girl says.

"What's that mean?" Emily and I both ask.

"You two are good to go!" the girl says. "Head on into your rooms and enjoy your seven minutes. Or just sit there. It's cool. Whatever."

Emily grins at me like she thinks I'm going to do terribly naughty things for the next seven minutes. Well, you know what? I'm not, Emily. And...

Oh no. What if Emily does terribly naughty things for

the next seven minutes? Daddy would be so mad at me if that happened. I'm supposed to keep an eye on her. Sort of, at least. I mean, I'm doing the worst job ever so far, and these dresses kind of prove that, but... we haven't been drinking so there's that?

That's about the only good thing I can say so far. We came to a frat party in super provocative outfits, sold ourselves to some guys at an auction, and now we're going to spend seven minutes alone with them in a room. And that's all just within the first thirty minutes of being here.

Um, seriously, what the heck? I'm so bad at this. I'm really sorry, Daddy. I didn't mean for this to happen!

The guy and girl next to us open the doors. He opens Emily's and she opens mine. My best friend waves bye to me and takes one step inside her room.

"Wait for me after and we can go back to the party together, alright?" Emily says before she goes all the way.

"It's seven minutes," I tell her. "I don't think either of us will have to--"

But I'm in the room now, and so is she. The door shuts behind me before I can finish talking.

And there I am, standing in a dark room, the lights set low. I blink through the darkness, adjusting, until I can sort of make out what's in here. There's... there's a bed. *Oh no, there's a bed.*

And then a chair right next to me. There's a chair on the other side of the room, too.

Sexy vampire dark prince superhero guy stares at me from across the room. I kind of smile and wave at him, like, oh, you know... hi, how are you?

"Um, how about we sit?" I say, grabbing onto the armrest of my chair. "We can talk?"

"Yeah, not a chance," he says, walking towards me. "No talking, Fiona. Not right now. You can try to explain this later if you want, but I'm not in the mood at the moment."

Oh no. I open my mouth to... to scream, I guess? And then they'll open the door?

I open my mouth, but then I shut it just as fast.

His voice sounds familiar. I thought it might have before when he bid on me, but the room we were in was so big and everyone was so loud that I figured it was just my imagination. I definitely recognize the way he talks now, though.

And... he knows my name...

GREY

Fiona's lucky I don't just spank her ass right here and now. I'm tempted. Real fucking tempted. The only reason I don't is because on the way to this room they gave us a huge speech about consent and making sure that anything that happens behind closed doors is acceptable and agreed upon by both people.

Well yeah, that's kind of fucking obvious, don't you think?

The point being that if I bend Fiona over the bed and spank her ass it's bound to get loud. Mostly from my hand smacking against her ass, but also she's been known to get, uh... a little exuberant? Seriously, it's the hottest thing I've ever heard. You haven't lived until the girl of your dreams is letting out little squeaks and yelps and moans when you spank her for being a bad girl.

It's not like I hurt her. I would *never* hurt Fiona. I mean, her ass probably stings a little afterwards, but she's also wetter than the inside of a bottle of water, so...

Also, let's take a step back for a second. As annoyed as I am about this whole frat party bullshit and the auction thing, I'm glad they take everything seriously and talk to people about consent and not being a huge fucking idiot. Everyone should be a decent human being, but some people just aren't, and those people deserve a massive punch to the face.

I'm still not very happy with this whole Sigma Epsilon Chi incident but I'll at least give credit where credit is due. They deserve a little credit. Not a lot, just a little. Charles is still here, even though I haven't seen the little shit, and... yeah, I'm wearing a mask, so I can kick his ass without getting into too much trouble afterwards.

I'm probably not going to do that, but I reserve the right to do it if he even so much as tries to talk to Emily and Fiona.

Anyways, let's get back to the matter at hand, which is Fiona and her impending punishment.

I step close to her while she watches me, her eyes trembling behind her white mask. She stares up at me, lips parted slightly, vague recognition in the way she looks at me.

Slow, I slide my fingers under her chin and tilt her head up slightly. I lean forward as if I'm about to kiss her and her eyes close instinctively, lips ready and waiting for mine.

"Fiona," I say, shaking my head, the barest hint of my lips brushing against hers. "Didn't you promise me you were going to be a good girl tonight?"

"I..." she says, eyes staying closed for a few seconds.

Then she opens them and looks at me, trying not to smile. Trying, yes, but she fails quickly. "Is that really you, Daddy?" she asks.

"Yes."

And then the entire concept of punishment just goes completely out the fucking window. Fiona kisses me, then she flings herself at me. She jumps onto me, legs wrapping around my waist like a fucking bug, and she clings to the nape of my neck with her hands. She rains kisses down on my cheeks and my nose and my lips, just everywhere, my entire face.

"Yay!" she squees, which isn't even a word, but somehow Fiona does it perfectly anyways. "Daddy!"

"You know how much trouble you're in?" I ask her while she dotes on me and almost makes me forget I ever wanted to punish her in the first place.

"Nope," she says, shaking her head in between kisses. "Please? I love you?"

"You love me, but you're a huge fucking brat and you're in trouble," I tell her.

"You love me, too, Daddy?" she asks, smiling at me, happy.

"I do love you, but you're still a brat and you're in trouble."

"How much trouble?" she asks.

"Well, let's see... about six minutes worth of trouble," I say, grinning. "I paid good money for this, so I think I should make it count."

"You can't spank me, though," she says, pouting. "It might be too loud."

"Yeah, and also you'd love it," I say, matter-of-fact. "We really need to work on this punishment thing. If I punish you with things you like, you're just going to keep getting into trouble, aren't you?"

"Nuh uh," she says, shaking her head fast. "I won't, I promise. You don't even have to punish me. I've learned my lesson, Daddy. But... I'm really happy you're here. Will you stay with me? All night? Will you be my date to the party? We can keep it a secret! I... I know that maybe we shouldn't keep secrets like that from Emily, but..."

I listen to her talk. She sounds so excited right now. And... it's this. This is what I wanted for her. I wanted her to be excited, but I just never thought she could be this excited over me. I don't know how to explain the way I feel about Fiona. There's too many raw emotions all mixed into one mess of contradiction.

It's like, yes, I want the best for her. I want her to have a good time growing up and learning and experiencing new things. But I also want to protect her and keep her safe and make sure she doesn't get hurt. That's the real issue with everything. Sometimes in order to experience new things we have to hurt ourselves. People can warn you all they want, but it's not the same.

How do you know the stove is hot if you don't touch it and find out? You're never going to know until you do, but once you do it you're never going to want to do it again, either. It's funny how that works.

But most of all, I want Fiona to be happy. I want to be happy, too, but I refuse to place my happiness over hers.

So far I don't have to, though. She's perfectly happy

with me. I don't know how that happened, it just did. I will never take her love for granted.

Fiona still needs to be punished, though. Sorry, baby girl, but your ass is mine. Or some other equivalent. We're going to figure this out.

Actually, now that I think about it...

"We're going to tell Emily soon," I tell her as she smiles at me, waiting for me to answer. "Not tonight. I'll stay with you, though. I'll be your date to the party. You're going to be a good girl the rest of the night, right?"

"Uh huh," she says, nodding fast. "Yes, Daddy. I'll be your good girl. I'll be a perfect little angel. See? I have white on and..."

Fiona realizes what she's drawing my attention to shortly after she says it. I take a moment to appreciate this for myself, though. It was one thing to see her flaunting herself on stage like that, but to see it up close and personal is something else entirely.

"Down," I say, smacking her butt as she clings to me. "Show me."

"You're mad," she says, pouting at me.

"Damn fucking right I'm mad," I say, shaking my head. "What the hell are you wearing?"

She grumbles and carefully unwraps her legs from around my waist and then lowers herself to the ground. Muttering about something or other, she takes a step back and lets me admire this provocative fucking bombshell of an outfit she's got on.

"Fiona, your breasts are practically falling out of your dress," I say, poking at the top of her cleavage.

"They're not falling out!" she protests. "It's... it's just got no straps so that's why it looks like that. It's a tube dress, Daddy."

"Yeah?" I ask. "You like this kind of clothing? You're going to start wearing it all the time when you go out? Because I think we're going to have some issues if that's the case."

"Not *all* the time..." she mumbles. "Emily picked it out. I knew you wouldn't like me wearing it here, but I thought that you'd like it when I came back to the hotel and you saw me in it. I don't like that woman, Daddy. The one who flirted with you at the front desk. She's older than me though, and I don't have any good dresses to wear for you, so I can see why you'd like her because--"

"Alright, going to stop you right there for a second," I say, holding up a finger to silence her. "I don't like Holly, I like you. Not only do I like you, but I love you, too. Now that we have that out of the way, I do think you look sexy as fuck in this dress, and if you want to wear outfits like this in private, then I would be more than happy to watch you skip around the house half naked. But that doesn't make you more of a woman to me, Fiona. If you want to get some nice dresses, we can go shopping and figure that out, alright?"

"I need money," she says, pouty. "I have a little and I've been trying to save up, but nice dresses cost a lot and I don't like asking you to buy me them. I know Emily probably used your money to buy this one, but that's different and I don't like that, either."

"If you want some dresses that you can wear that are

nice, and not, uh... you know, your breasts popping out all over the fucking place, then we're going to figure that out and get you some dresses, alright? Stop being stubborn."

"No!" she says, defiant and grinning. Seriously, what a fucking brat. "I like being stubborn with you, Daddy. Only sometimes, though. Just a little bit, alright?"

"Fine, but we're getting you a fucking dress, and if you fight me on this I'm going to spank your ass."

"Can you spank my ass anyways?" she asks.

"Yes, but... so besides your breasts, uh... Fiona, this dress is too much."

"Do you mean like... *this?*"

She does a cute little spin, facing away from me, and then she just kind of does this thing where she pops her ass back at me, showing off her curves. And, yeah, holy fuck does this girl have curves.

I can't help myself. It's instinct by now, raw and real. I reach out and run my palm along the side of her hip and down, feeling every beautiful inch of her delicious ass. You have no idea how much I want to hear my palm clap against her backside right now, but I restrain myself and leave her with a light, nowhere near satisfying, little slap.

"Daddy, I wish you could--" she starts to say, but I'm not through with her yet.

I grab her hips with both hands and pull her back towards me in one smooth motion. My right hand slips to the front, resting tight against her lower stomach, and my left hand slides towards the bottom of her dress. I lift it up, revealing everything inch of her from her waist down.

She squirms against me, fighting for a half second, but

MIA CLARK

as soon as she realizes what I'm doing she leans back, gasping, breathing hard.

"Daddy, what are you--?" she whispers.

"Take this off," I tell her, tugging at the waistband of panties that are far too thin. "Is this a thong, Fiona?"

"Um..." she says, cheeks red. "Kind of?"

"Kind of?" I ask, because apparently this needs to be asked.

"I didn't want to wear it."

"So you were going to come to the party without panties on?"

"Noooo!" she protests. "It's... it's because if you have a dress like this and you wear regular panties you'll get panty lines, and I would have still done that, but I guess people would have noticed and stared at my butt then, and I wasn't going to go around without any underwear on at all, because I really was trying to be a good girl, Daddy, so..."

"I appreciate your explanation," I tell her. "Why are these still on you, though? Do you remember what I asked you, baby girl?"

"Uh huh," she says. "Yes, Daddy. You told me to take them off."

"Good girl," I tell her, leaning close to kiss her neck. "Hurry up, baby, because we don't have a lot of time left."

"Yes, Daddy..."

24

FIONA

Seeing Daddy flipped a switch in me. I came into this room expecting to ignore the guy who "bought" me at the auction. No one can buy me, though! I'm not for sale, because I belong to Daddy, and...

I mean, Daddy's here, so everything worked out perfectly, right?

Yup, um... a little, except I've got one teensy tiny problem now...

Like I said, seeing Daddy flipped a switch in me. I think maybe it's a dial instead of a switch, though. One you can keep turning up and up, you know? Mine was at zero before I knew Daddy was here, and then it went to a solid five after I figured it out. Ten's probably the highest, but right now my dial feels like it's at an eleven or a twelve.

And what's that mean exactly? Yup, um...

I shimmy my skirt up so I can easily remove my panties for Daddy just like he asked. He watches me intently and I hesitate. He clears his throat while he stares at my thong and I suddenly feel super embarrassed for no reason. I mean, I've removed my panties for Daddy before, right? Yup, obviously, except none of those times were ever like this.

Blushing, my cheeks lighting up the room with how red they are, I reach for the thin straps of my thong, the ones resting on my hips, and I slowly peel them down my legs. Daddy watches, and then his straight face turns into a wicked grin.

They're stuck. Not that stuck. I can remove them. Except that I'm wetter than I thought possible considering we haven't even been doing anything. My arousal soaks through the front of my thong and the tiny patch of cloth clings to my pussy as I try to pull my panties down and take them off for Daddy.

They come off, but not without a little bit of a fight. My pussy is completely drenched by my arousal and I leave a trail of slickness down my thighs as I finally give in to Daddy's demands. Once I have my thong around my ankles, I step out of it gingerly and then stand up, clinging to the tiny little thing.

Daddy holds out his hand, palm up. "Those are mine," he says with a devilish grin. "You won't be wearing them for the rest of the night."

I nod and say nothing, simply looking down at Daddy's feet while I hand over my panties that now look far too small to ever have even fit on me. He takes them, his fingers glistening from my arousal as he carefully bunches up my thong and stuffs it into his pocket.

"Now..." Daddy says, just one word, slow and languorous.

Oh no. There's more? We don't have that much time in here so I'm not sure what we're going to do, though. Is he going to punish me? Um, I wouldn't really mind...

Spank me? Please, Daddy...?

"On the bed," he tells me. "Crawl up on your hands and knees. Keep your skirt up just like that, baby girl. Get so that your ass is just about even with the side of the bed and stay there."

"Yes, Daddy," I say, nodding quick.

I hurry to the edge of the bed and place my hands on it, then I climb up and crawl forward until my pussy and the curves of my butt are on open display for him. I don't look back, but I can tell Daddy's staring at me, looking at the wetness he brought on. I'm completely soaked and embarrassed and I'm pretty sure if I stay like this for much longer I'm going to drip on the bed and leave a massive wet spot.

To be fair, Daddy and I usually leave wet spots in a lot of places, but I'm really not sure how I feel about leaving one here. This isn't my bed. It's not Daddy's bed, either. I have no idea whose bed this is, actually. Are they going to know? I don't see how they wouldn't figure it out!

So basically I'm leaving a wet spot on some stranger's bed and there's no possible way they won't know it's from me. This room was reserved for Daddy and I after the auction, so...

I hear something, but I'm too caught up in my own

imagination to realize what it is. I figure it out real quick, though. *Zip.* Yup, that's a zipper. And then something else.

That's... that's a cock.

Oh my gosh.

Daddy comes up behind me, his cock hard and perfectly lined up with my pussy. He stands there, the head just barely tapping against my arousal-slick slit. I can feel him jump a little, his cock throbbing as he comes so incredibly close to pushing himself inside me. He doesn't, though. He stays just like that, stands just far enough away that we aren't together but we're still touching.

"Are you ready for your punishment?" Daddy asks me.

"I'm really sorry, Daddy," I say before burying my face in the blankets in front of me on the bed.

"I'm glad you're sorry but I'm still going to punish you," he says, firm.

"I know," I tell him, pouting, my voice muffled in the blankets.

"You aren't going to enjoy this," he says, with a hint of mystery and intrigue in his voice. "That's not entirely true. The point is to enjoy it, but not too much."

"I don't understand?" I say to him.

"I'm going to step forward, baby girl," he says, gentle. "Ready?"

Before I can answer, Daddy does exactly what he said. When he steps forward, his cock pushes inside me, filling me. I let out a murmured gasp but I don't know how loud I can be, so I hold most of my excitement in. I squeeze tight against the blankets as Daddy thrusts all the way inside me. I'm beyond wet so it's not exactly hard for him to do, either. Even still, Daddy's a perfect fit, his cock throbbing deep in my tight little pussy.

I used to think I might be too small for Daddy to fit himself inside me, but over time I realized that we're just perfect together. Not too big, not too small, but just right...

"Now what I want you to do," Daddy says, this time with a mischievous smirk sneaking into his words, "is to press your chest right up against the bed to help yourself stay balanced. You're going to reach between your legs with one hand and play with yourself. Do it good, baby girl. I want you to try to make yourself cum as quickly as possible, but--and here's where your punishment comes in--under no circumstances are you to actually cum. You can get close, you can feel like you're about to at any second, but if you make yourself cum then you're in even more trouble later. Understand?"

I nod and quickly shove one hand between my thighs as I get into position for Daddy. I'm already teasing myself, building myself up to a quick orgasm, and I nearly go over the edge a few seconds in but finally stop myself.

"Um, Daddy?" I ask, trying to distract myself before I go way too far overboard. I never knew how hot this could be, and now I feel kind of stupid for not realizing it before.

"Yes, Fiona?" Daddy answers.

"I can't cum, right?" I ask him.

"That's correct," he tells me.

"But... can I make you cum?"

"You want me to cum?" he asks me, smirking as he

lays one palm on the upper curve of my ass, fingers resting on my hiked up dress.

"A little bit," I say, lying to myself. "Or... a lot... please, Daddy?"

"You won't have your panties for the rest of the night," he reminds me. "I'm not going to pull out, either. If you make me cum, I'm going to cum inside you, and you're going to have me leaking out of you the rest of the night while we're at the party. Whenever we dance, whenever we go to get a drink, even when we're just standing around talking..."

Oh... oh my God... that's...

My fingers tease and touch my clit just like Daddy told me, but his reminder of what will happen if I make him cum inside me does more than any physical touch ever could right now. Is that what I want? A naughty little reminder of what Daddy and I did when we were in this room for seven minutes together, alone? How much more time do we have, though? Can I make him cum before we have to leave?

I rock back and forth, grinding up and down on Daddy's cock. He shifts behind me, his fingers digging roughly into the soft curve of my ass. I toy with my clit with two fingers, first stroking up and down fast to get myself close, and then slowly circling around. Daddy's precious little pearl, that's what I like to think of my clit as.

Just for him! I hope he likes it...

My pussy spasms, nearly sending me over the edge into an orgasm, but I stave it off quick and go back to normal. Except I'm so incredibly tight and worked up at the moment that I don't know how much longer I can last. I...

"Daddy...?" I whimper, moving my hips, sliding up and down his cock. "How... how much time do we...?"

"Around three minutes," he says, his words coming out as more of a grunt. "You feel so good, baby girl. I can feel you. You really want to cum, don't you?"

"Uh huh, I do, but..."

"I'll more than make it up to you when we get back to the hotel, alright?" he says, softly patting my butt with one hand.

He shifts his other hand to my hip, holding me lightly, letting me do all of the work of punishing myself by denying my own orgasm.

This is either the best or the worst punishment. I'm practically gushing, fully ready to go, but... I can't. I can't do it! That thought and that alone is what somehow keeps me sane. Well, I mean, that and the fact that Daddy told me he's going to give me the orgasm of a lifetime when we get back to the hotel.

Seriously, I don't even know if I'll be able to survive that one. I'm going crazy already, so if Daddy makes me go even crazier later, um...

Yes, please? Yes, I want Daddy to make me an incoherent, blubbering mess while he teases orgasm after orgasm out of my body back at our fancy hotel room.

And that nearly sends me over the edge, too. I pause, because I'm pretty sure even a slight breeze would bring me to orgasm right now. I can't even explain this. My mind is mush. I'm so wet and aroused that it hurts, but the best possible hurt in the entire world. And I could orgasm at any second, but I can't orgasm because Daddy told me not to.

It's like my orgasm keeps building and building, over and over, but at the last possible second I hold back, keep myself from going over the edge. And that's great, except then I realize there's another cliff to climb and I've never been up here, never gone this far, and...

Daddy's cock throbs and pulses inside me. Oh no. If there's one thing I know, it's that I get extra excited and aroused whenever Daddy cums inside me. It's like that's my moment of glory, and if I haven't already cum that always sends me over the edge. Even if I've already cum for him before, sometimes I'll just cum again out of the blue because of how sexy I feel after making Daddy feel so amazing that he just *needs* to cum for me.

This is a serious problem at the moment. I need to be good. I wasn't good, and this is Daddy's way of punishing me, and I need to be good. I mean, I wasn't exactly a terribly bad and naughty girl, either. I get why Daddy's a little upset, but I don't think he's too upset, either.

He's...

I don't have time to go over this in my mind anymore. I stop completely, my fingers barely touching my clit because any amount of extra sensation is going to completely obliterate me right now. Daddy cums inside me over and over again, practically an endless amount, jet after jet of his sticky sweet seed filling my pussy. I can feel every part of him, his throbbing cock, each pulsing vein, every last drop of his cum.

My body is begging me for release. It's not even like it would be hard, either. Just a little... *touch*... right *there*...

I could. I could make myself. I probably could by complete accident if I'm being honest. It takes full and measured control not to cum right now even though my mind and my body are screaming at me to just... just do... a little...

It gets even worse when Daddy keeps pumping inside me. His orgasm is mostly done now, but his cock lets out these light spasms every few seconds and I can practically feel every last drop of his cum splashing inside of me.

And if I thought *that* was bad, it gets even worse still. He's filled me so utterly and completely that there's nowhere else for it to go but out. Daddy's sticky white cream slowly slides out of my pussy and down my thighs, heading towards the wet spot I'm sure I left on the bed already.

Yup... everyone's going to know what we did in here...

I don't know if that's incredibly embarrassing or stupidly hot. It's incredibly stupidly embarrassingly hot? I guess that's a thing and I'm only just now realizing how much of one it is sometimes.

I don't think I'd want to make this a common, everyday occurrence, but...

"One last touch," Daddy tells me. "Show me that you can keep yourself under control for me, baby girl."

I whimper and whine and fight with every inch of my being. I can't. I don't want to. I don't trust myself, Daddy! I...

Slowly but surely, I press my fingers hard against my

clit. It's too much. I'm too sensitive. I'm not even moving and I think I'm about to cum. My clit trembles under my touch, almost like how Daddy's cock felt when he was cumming inside me. Just a little piece of that, though. My clit is obviously much smaller than Daddy's cock, but for some reason I feel like everything I just felt from him is about to happen to me.

To finish this off, to prove to myself and to Daddy what a good girl I am, I slide my fingers up and down my clit one last time. My entire body shakes and I think I went too far. I'm going to cum. I completely misjudged what I was doing. I don't know why I did that. Why did I do that?

I'm so so so so so so so sorry, Daddy!

I'm...

My body spasms and shakes and I think I'm about to cum at any second, to give in to my orgasm, but somehow I manage to keep hold of myself. Daddy slides out of me and that nearly sends me over the edge, too, but... no, I survive. I make it. I keep everything under control. I...

I fall onto the bed, unable to think of anything but having an orgasm and also not having an orgasm. Where am I and what am I doing? These thoughts, those answers, it's too much to fathom right now. I need to stop, need to calm myself, I need to...

Someone knocks at the door.

"Fifteen seconds!" a girl shouts to us through the closed door. "Whatever you're doing, hurry it up. I'm not waiting. You better be ready when this door opens."

I stand on wobbly legs and nearly fall over, but Daddy catches me and keeps me up. His cock bounces in front of me, still hard even after how much I felt him cum. My first instinct is to reach out and touch it and to hold his shaft, which... I mean, I do that. I hold Daddy's cock tight in my hand, squeezing slightly.

I like it. This is mine. I'm Daddy's and Daddy is mine.

"Good girl," Daddy says, smiling and kissing my forehead.

"Thank you, Daddy," I whisper to him, soft and sweet.

"You're going to have to let go of that. I need to zip up. You need to pull your dress down, too."

Daddy gently slides my fingers off of his shaft and then somehow manages to stuff his throbbing cock back into his pants, behind his boxer briefs, and zips everything up. I stand there in a stupor, completely oblivious of the fact that my dress is still hiked up around my waist.

Daddy grins at me, pulls my panties from his pocket, and then carefully wipes up as much of the mess between my thighs as he can. Once he's done, he quickly pulls my dress down and covers me up again.

Just in time, too. Three quick knocks on the door and then someone opens it wide. I stare at them, blinking, still confused.

Ummmm... yup.

Daddy wraps up my panties in a handful of tissues he found on a little table next to the bed and then covertly stuffs everything back into his pocket.

"You two look like you had fun..." someone says.

"Uh huh," I say, nodding stupidly, which is apparently funny because then they laugh.

I can't even focus right now. I have no idea if the

person who opened the door is a guy or a girl. Maybe it's two people, one of each. Who knows?

I need a nap.

Daddy takes my hand and squeezes it tight and I look up at him. Yes, thank you, Daddy. I'll be your good girl. Always! Forever, too. Please, if you'll let me?

I will follow Daddy anywhere, too. Anywhere and everywhere. He holds my hand tight and leads me out of the room. My first step is slow, a little wobbly, but I find my footing quickly after that and I gain confidence at Daddy's side.

I don't even know what just happened but it was amazing.

25

—

GREY

—

H*oly fucking shit.* Those are the best words right now. Probably the only words I'll need for awhile.

Look, I get that Fiona wanted to come out and have fun with Emily. I completely understand that part of this. How did they wind up on some makeshift stage in a frat house being sold to the highest bidder, though? Who the hell thought that was a good idea? I need to dig down deep and figure out what the fuck was going on there, but I'm not in the mood right now.

If I'm being super honest, I'm in the mood to toss Fiona over my shoulder, carry her ass all the way back to the hotel, and make good on my promise to her. I kind of want to make her suffer a little more, though. Not in a bad way. It's just impossibly hot watching her stumble around, her legs quivering as if she's forgotten how to walk.

Yeah, I did that to her. I mean, technically she did it to herself, but it was my idea. That... fuck... that was probably my best punishment to date.

There's something I forgot, though. I didn't forget it so much as we had to vacate our little slice of heaven to soon. We leave the room hand in hand, Fiona clinging to me like she can't possibly do this alone. I don't want her to, either. I want to be here with her every step of the way. I thought it'd be a good idea to let her have this night to herself, to experience something new and different with Emily, but I guess I didn't fully realize how much she wanted me to be here with her.

It's hard, you know? I want her to be her own person, but I also want to cuddle the fuck out of her and spend every waking moment at her side. What the fuck am I supposed to do in that case? No fucking clue. I'm still trying to figure it out. I've never felt this way about anyone before, but I've always felt a strong connection to Fiona. I just, uh... yeah... she's my sister's best friend and she's twelve years younger than me so I kind of pushed all thoughts of anything out of my head before they could take hold of me.

She's got a hold on me now, though. Literally and figuratively. She holds my arm tight as I escort her into the hall and we wait for Emily.

Which, speaking of...

"Oh no!" Fiona says, gasping, eyes wide, staring at the door down the hall from the one we just came out of. "Daddy, um... Emily's... she's with a guy in there, and... oh no..."

I smirk, wondering how I should let this play out. I mean, let's be real for a second, these girls really should have thought this through better. You get involved in a Seven Minutes in Heaven auction and at some point you sort of have to realize you're going to wind up in a room alone with a strange guy. What's the worst that can happen? I don't think I have to answer that question.

In this case, nothing bad's going to happen. Nothing bad did happen. Except I really do want Fiona to realize that bad things can happen in life and you sort of need to always be aware of that. I mean, don't let it go too far, don't let those thoughts get out of control and stop you from living and enjoying your life, but...

She frets and fidgets and looks like she's ready to just run down the hall, fling the door open, and beat up some guy that's doing who knows what to her best friend, my little sister. I lay a reassuring hand on her arm and rub her shoulder.

"It's fine," I tell her. "It's just Porter in there. He's a good kid."

"Who's Porter?" Fiona asks me, head tilted sideways.

I shrug. "I just met him. Him and his friends were stuck outside. We figured out how to sneak in here together. Honestly, out of all of them, he's probably the only one I would have trusted to go in there with Emily. The other two are cool, but Porter didn't even want to go in so I trust him more and I don't have to deal with some guys ogling my little sister, you know? It's a win-win from what I can tell."

Fiona looks up at me, brow furrowed. She purses her lips and makes a little harrumph sound, like I probably should have told her all this earlier so she wouldn't worry over nothing. But then her eyes dart towards the door again and I can tell she's still worried no matter what I say.

And... I mean... Porter seems like a good kid, but admittedly I don't know him that well so...

Sometimes you just have to hope for the best. Emily knows how to take care of herself. I'd like to think I taught her at least that much over the years. They're also running this whole auction thing pretty strict so that makes me feel slightly better.

Slightly. Don't fuck this up, Porter. I know we helped each other get in here, but so help me God if you do anything to hurt my little sister...

Less than a minute later, while Fiona and I are staring at the door waiting for someone to do something and open it, it just kind of opens on its own. Some guy standing outside nods and then I see Porter and my little sister come waltzing out of the room together.

That's not entirely accurate. Emily waltzes out of the room, happy as can be, but Porter looks like he's headed to some kind of trial by combat. His face is pale, eyes sullen, like his entire world is about to end. Emily grabs his hand and tugs him down the hallway to where Fiona and I are standing. Porter, to his credit, looks both intrigued and afraid for his life at the fact that he's currently holding my sister's hand.

Which is exactly how it should be. Good job, dude.

Fiona just keeps clinging to me, completely forgetting that we probably shouldn't be this close and cuddly in front of Emily. She belatedly realizes what's going on and her eyes widen in panic as Emily glances from her to me, my sister watching as Fiona squeezes her arms tight around mine.

"So... who's this?" Emily asks, sizing me up, suspicious.

I clear my throat, hoping to pull off some sort of gruff, deep voice that she won't recognize, but Fiona sneaks in quick and intercepts me.

"You know we aren't supposed to tell anyone our real names here, Alice!" Fiona says, sticking her tongue out, apparently using some fake name her and my sister came up with.

"So you're saying you don't know his name?" Emily asks, doubly suspicious.

"I mean, I know it, but I'm not going to tell you because it's against the rules."

"I guess," Emily grumbles, partially admitting defeat. "What am I supposed to call him, then? Doesn't he remind you of Grey? It's really weird. I don't know..."

I cock my head to the side. I can do this. I've decided sticking to one word answers is my safest bet.

"Who?" I ask, my voice rough and rugged.

I mean, let's be real, I'm pretty rough and rugged to begin with, but there's always room for improvement. I could be a lumberjack, for example. Never really wanted to be one before, but that's my inspiration for the night. Some rough and rugged college student who also just so happens to be a lumberjack.

Look, don't even ask. I have no idea how this works. I'm making it up as I go along.

"He's, um..." Fiona says, mind whirring with possibilities. "Dave?"

I nod. Yeah, sure, let's go with that. I can't say I've ever wanted to be a Dave before, but one night of it won't hurt.

"Dave..." Emily says, biting her bottom lip and giving me a suspicious look. "I guess. Um, so... this is..."

"Rupert," Porter says, winging it.

Nice. I like it. He even got most of the letters of his real name in there. Good job, Porter.

"Rupert?" Emily asks, giggling. "You really want to go with that one?"

"Yeah, why not?" Porter says with a shrug.

"I like it," Fiona says, grinning. "It sounds fun."

"Oh, Rupert is definitely fun..." Emily says, as vague as possible.

Porter's eyes flash and he looks up at me like I'm about to murder him. I can't say I won't, either. It was nice knowing you Porter, but this is my sister we're talking about, so...

"We kissed!" Emily says, like she's just revealed something super scandalous.

Porter closes his eyes, waiting for my deathblow. It doesn't come, because... I mean, they kissed? I don't know. I'm protective of my little sister but I don't think I can murder someone in good conscience over a kiss. Also, from the sound of it she instigated this, so I can't blame him now can I?

I mean, I *can*. I'm not saying I'll never blame a guy if

my sister kisses him first. I'm just saying that in this case I'm going to accept the fact that Porter likely didn't want to kiss her because he knew I was right here. So... if he did kiss her, it was probably under Emily's duress, except also, look, I want her to be happy, so...

Don't fuck this up, Porter. Make my little sister happy. Not too happy. Keep this shit PG-13 or something.

"Rupert's, um... he's a little shy, I think?" Emily offers. "We talked, too! Oh, he's in the same degree program as me. Isn't that cool? We can be study buddies!"

I raise one eyebrow, staring at my new friend.

"Uh, just studying!" Porter says quick. "Not, uh... you know... it's not like that."

"What about kissing?" Emily asks, pouting at him. "You didn't like kissing me?"

Oh shit. I'm sorry, dude. This is the question of a lifetime. Answer carefully.

"I did, but... I just meant... I think we should get to know each other better, too?"

"Well, yeah," Emily says as if this is obvious. "Which is also why you should ask me on a date in between our study sessions together."

"And kissing," Fiona adds, because she's being a huge brat. Seriously, I'm tempted to just bend her over my knee and spank her right here and now, except, you know, the fact that my sister is right next to us sort of puts a damper on that.

"So we study, and if we do good we kiss a little, and then we go on dates when we don't have to study, and then..."

"How about we go on a date now?" Porter asks, saving himself. "There's a party going on and we're all standing in this hallway talking when we could be dancing and having fun."

Good job, Porter. I like the way you think. I don't know how I feel about the way Emily thinks.

Like, let's just go with this for a second, alright? Hypothetically speaking how many study dates and regular dates until we get to the x-rated "and then..." that Emily just mentioned?

I think fifty is a good number. Fifty to start, but probably fifty more after that. Let's make it a good and even five hundred. Five hundred dates and then, if everything's fine and dandy up to that point, then Emily and Porter can come talk to me about having sex. Except I'll say no, of course. Wait until you're married. Not just newly married, either. Maybe your five year anniversary. Make it real special, right?

I know I'm being unreasonable. I don't care.

Fiona cares and she somehow knows what I'm thinking, so she becomes a huge brat, playfully stomps on my foot, and glares at me with a silly face.

"I think you two look really cute together," she says to Porter and Emily. "I bet Daddy would be super happy if you both started dating, too. He was talking to me about that kind of thing the other day, actually."

I was? Hey, don't do this to me, Fiona. You're supposed to be on my side.

And, I mean, we *have* talked about that kind of thing, I guess. Not in any specific terms. It's more of a "Would you mind if Emily dated in college?" and I say, "Uh, yeah, college guys are awful, she can't do that." Then Fiona tells me that all college guys can't be awful. There's got to be some good ones. And I admit there might be, but only like... maybe one in the entire college.

And here he is. Porter. The one nice guy in Emily's entire college. Why did I set them up? I'm really pissed off at myself now. I have no one to blame but me. Fuck.

"Who's Daddy?" Porter asks, confused. He turns to Emily, who is still happily holding his hand. "Your dad?"

"Um, that's kind of a long story," Emily says, unsure how to proceed. "My parents died when I was little, and I don't want you to think I'm getting deep here. I don't really remember it too well. But my older brother, Grey, he took care of me and he's kind of been like my dad all these years so I call him Daddy and... Fiona does too, because he's nice to her and she doesn't really have anyone and Grey likes taking care of her."

Which is true. I've just never heard my sister explain it that way before. I like taking care of Fiona? She's always made sure to remind me that I need to take care of Fiona. Take care of Fiona, Daddy! But I've never heard her say that she thought I liked it?

It just kind of makes me question some things. Mainly, uh... what does my sister know? Does she suspect something? Ugh. This is complicated.

Maybe Fiona and I should talk to her about all this soon. Not right now. I don't want to ruin my little sister's attempt at being a rebel and going to a frat party. Soon, though. Sometime after this weekend is over.

"Can we dance now?" Fiona asks, hopping up and down, still clinging to me. "I want to dance with Dave! He's so fun and nice and amazing, Emily."

"Oh yeah?" Emily asks, grinning. "Better be careful, Dave. If you think Daddy's protective of me, you should see how he treats Fiona."

Fiona blushes and mumbles and shakes her head fast. "Noooo! He's way more protective of you than he is of me."

"Which is why you live with him and you two go everywhere together."

"Because I'm helping!" Fiona protests. "I need to help out around the house or he'll think I'm taking advantage of him."

"*Su~re...*" Emily says, sarcasm dripping from her words like thick syrup. "I'm going to tell Daddy about Dave tomorrow. Let's see how that goes."

I shrug and grin right now, but... shit. What the fuck am I supposed to do tomorrow? Should I get mad at this made up Dave person or what? But Dave is me. Can I be mad at myself?

Sure, why not? I don't know. I'll figure it out when we get there.

"Dance!" Fiona says, bratty. "Please!"

I love her. I love her even when she's a huge fucking brat like she is right now.

I also love the fact that she seems to have forgotten that I'm going to be leaking out of her all night and dancing really isn't going to help that fact...

That's secondary, though. I just love Fiona and I'm

happy I get to be here with her tonight, even if it's under odd circumstances and we can't exactly be open with everyone about the entire truth at the moment.

"Let's go," I say, nodding to everyone, full force with my rough and rugged lumberjack voice.

26

FIONA

I get so caught up in the excitement of having Daddy at the party with me that I kind of completely forget about some of the things I probably shouldn't be forgetting about?

Mainly, Daddy starts playing dirty as soon as we get on the dance floor. I don't know if this is what they mean by dirty dancing, but I think it could be. Also it's not so much a dance floor as it is the main room that we first came in when Emily and I stood on the stage to get auctioned off to the highest bidder.

Which ended up being Daddy. Yay! And Rupert, who Daddy told me is really Porter, and I guess he's nice? Emily seems to be having a fun time with him, at least.

Anyways, about that dirty dancing...

I spin and dance with Daddy, but then he pulls me close and we grind together a little. It's not lewd or too scandalous, but it's just dancing, you know? Daddy pulls me close and I look up into his eyes and we're dancing, but then his leg's between mine and I grin because we've never danced like this in public before.

And then his thigh grinds against my clit because, you know, we're dancing really close, and...

I haven't had an orgasm yet. I was a good girl, Daddy! Which is great to say, but now I'm worked up and oversensitive. I shudder and my eyes roll into the back of my head as Daddy and I dance together. He holds me tight, hiding my sudden rush of ecstasy from everyone around us. I think I could cum right here and now on the dance floor if Daddy really wanted me too.

The song comes to an end and we slowly pull away from each other but we stay close after, too. I don't want to leave Daddy's side at all tonight. I'm going to stay with him no matter what!

I tug on his arm and he leans down so I can whisper to him. I don't think he expects me to say what I do, though.

"You could make me cum really easily right here if you keep dancing with me like that," I tell him, truthful.

His eyes grow wide and he looks at me a little differently now. An excited different, though, like this thought hadn't occurred to him before I said it and now he's seriously considering it...

I beg him with my eyes. *Please, Daddy...*

He grins at me and shakes his head.

"Not here," he whispers back. "I like you loud, Fiona. You can't do that if we're in here, now can you? I don't want to tease you too much, though. We're just having fun right now. If it seems too much like a punishment then let me know and I'll ease back a little, alright?"

"Nope," I say, shaking my head. "I like it. I'll be good, Daddy. I'll tell you, alright? If it's too much. You can tease me. But, um... you said it'll be extra good when we get back to the hotel room?"

"As much as you want, baby girl," he says, kissing my forehead.

"I want you," I say, blushing. "I... I can still feel you inside me..."

Daddy grins and glances down between us. Yup... I might need to go to the bathroom to clean up soon. Again. So far so good, though. Daddy really did cum a lot. I like it. *Mmm...*

"Hey, get a room, you two!" Emily says, rushing over with Porter as soon as the next song starts. "Oh, wait, you already did!"

She keeps telling that joke, but I kind of like it. Daddy and I got a room here, with our Seven Minutes in Heaven auction, but we also have a room at the hotel, so it's like two rooms? We needed to get a room so bad we ended up with two. That thought makes me laugh and I start to giggle. I can't exactly tell Emily the real reason why, but she grins when I laugh at her joke.

They look cute together, too. Her and Porter. They aren't dancing like Daddy and I are, or at least not most of the time. I try to distract Daddy, but every so often he looks over at the two of them and if he thinks Porter is a little too close to Emily he kind of grunts and glares and then I have to distract him even more so that Emily doesn't realize what's going on.

Because, really now, Daddy, why would some guy I

just met at a frat party who is *supposed* to be super into me start glaring at Emily when she's dancing close to his friend? I'm not an expert on masquerade parties and sneaking around, but pretty sure that's the worst way to go about it. Just saying.

Mostly this all goes well but then Emily has this great idea of her and Porter sneaking over to the alcohol table and grabbing a couple drinks when no one's looking. It's only beer, and unless she drinks a ton I think she'll be fine, but I basically need the strength of God to hold Daddy back from going berserk and dragging Emily out of the party.

"Stop!" I say, clinging to him for all the good it does me; not very much, by the way. He starts dragging me along with him. "Down boy! Be good! Woof!"

"What, am I a dog now?" he asks, being a huge grump. "Thanks, Fifi..."

"Hey!" I say, laughing and slapping playfully at his arm. "I'm not a dog, either. I'm Daddy's Little Angel..."

"You *are* dressed in all white," he says, taking a second to admire my sexy outfit.

I tug on his arm until he comes close. Blushing, I whisper to him, "Once you get me out of this dress later will you cover me in all white, too?"

"Fiona..." Daddy says, staring hard at me, lust in his eyes, a growl in his voice.

"Yes, Daddy?" I ask, acting sweet and innocent.

"You're done for once we get out of here. You know that, right?"

"Uh huh..." I say, nodding quick.

"Good girl," he says, grinning and pulling me in for a kiss.

A real kiss this time. Not just a kiss on the cheek. Daddy and I dance and sway to the music but we aren't trying to be dirty dancers anymore. We're just dancing and having fun and kissing. I like being with Daddy and this is kind of like our first date together? The first one where we went out together and didn't have to hide anything, at least.

We're hiding behind masks and pretending that Daddy is someone else entirely, but still. I like that we were able to do this together.

"Gertrude!" Emily says, rushing over with a pair of red plastic cups. "Look! I got you one, too."

Porter follows alongside her, also with two cups. He stands stock still for the longest time, Emily completely oblivious at his side, and then slowly stretches out his hand and offers Daddy one of the cups.

Daddy looks like he's going to start a war. I'm trying to help, though. I can do this, Daddy! We can be good, I promise.

I mean, I'm pretty sure that three out of the four of us right here are underage and we really shouldn't be drinking anything, but, um... I don't know how to get Emily to realize that in front of Daddy without blowing his cover completely, so...

"We can't drink more than this," I tell her, putting on my best responsible voice. "Daddy would get upset if he found out and he let us come to this party together even though he was really worried about it, so we should be good."

"I guess," Emily says, pouting at me. "If we don't make him angry he'll let us come to more parties, huh?"

"Right!" I say.

I don't even have to look over at Daddy to see that he completely disagrees with all of this but he's willing to accept the lesser of two evils.

Porter looks relieved, too. His friends show up, which I guess they're also Daddy's friends now? They've got their own red cups and they raise them high in the air like some sort of beer salute.

"Yeah!" Wyatt shouts over the music. He's the loud one.

"Thanks for helping us get into this party, Grey," Holden adds.

Daddy and I freeze. *Oh no*. We both look over towards Emily but she doesn't seem to have noticed what they said. Porter elbows his friend hard in the side.

"Oh, uh..."

"Guys, why aren't you cheersing?" Emily asks, taking a good hard look at everyone's cups. She holds hers up high like Wyatt and Holden. "Come on! Cheers!"

We each take our cups and lift them up. Daddy smiles over at me and gives me a little nod. Just this once, at least until I'm twenty-one. I tap the rim of my cup against Daddy's cup first, and then I do the same with Emily and eventually we've all tapped each of our cups together.

I take a sip. This is my first taste of beer. I can't believe this. I...

I make a funny face as I swallow. I don't know what I expected, but I sort of thought it'd be more... I don't know, good? I don't get it. Why do people drink this?

Daddy takes a sharp swig of his own drink, downing it like he's done this a million times before. I guess he has, too. I mean, I don't know about a million times, but I know Daddy drinks with his work and business friends sometimes when he goes to business meetings.

After he swallows, he looks over at me. He smiles at first, then he breaks out laughing.

"What?" I ask, hands on my hips, glaring at him, acting silly.

"Your face. Wow. I..."

"I happen to like my face!" I say, sticking my tongue out at him.

"Me too," he says, sneaking in quick and giving me a kiss, tongue and all. "You don't like the beer, huh?"

"It's... um... is it always like that? It's got a weird taste."

"Nah, this is just cheap stuff," he says. "It's fine if you want to get drunk, but the good stuff tastes better. Which you'll find out when you're old enough to drink..."

He ends with a quick shake of his head and an exaggerated sigh.

"Pft!" I murmur, sticking my tongue out again.

"You aren't our dad or anything, Dave!" Emily says, coming to my unnecessary defense. "How old are you anyways?"

Uh oh...

Also, I mean, Daddy kind of is like our dad which is why we call him Daddy? It's not exactly the same, and he's nowhere near my real father. I don't even know who my real father is, so...

"Shush," I tell my best friend. "He's just teasing me. It's true, though. Maybe once we're older we can go to a nice place and Daddy can get us good drinks."

"Yes!" Emily says after she takes another sip of her nasty beer and makes a weird face. "Are you inviting Dave, too? Are you two a thing now?"

"Um, we won't be twenty-one for over two years, Emily, so I don't think I have to figure out if Dave and I are a thing yet."

"Alice!" Emily says, whispering harshly. "Don't blow my cover here!"

After that she steals Porter away so they can dance again. They don't go very far, just a few steps out, but they look like they're having fun. Porter seems like a nice guy. Wyatt and Holden keep trying to dance with any girl who comes within a foot of them, which, um... I don't know how that's going. They seem nice, but I think they're trying a little too hard.

And then here I am with Daddy! We're dancing, too. Daddy takes my cup from me and pours it into his. We dance and hold each other and sway and enjoy the night. He takes a sip every now and then, but I'm perfectly content just getting drunk off of having Daddy with me. I definitely like the taste of Daddy more than I like the taste of cheap beer, too.

"I love you," I whisper to him during a slow song when we're extra close.

"I love you, too, baby girl," he whispers back, kissing my ear.

That's how the party goes. It's how it ends, too. Little by little, people start to leave, until there's barely anyone left in the frat house. Everyone in our group makes their way outside. Emily didn't even drink more than that one cup of beer, but she starts to sway like she's had way too much to drink. I think she's doing it so that she can cuddle closer to Porter, though. She wraps one arm around his shoulder and he steadies her with his hand tight around her hip.

I cling to Daddy as we walk down the hall and back to the front door. He keeps his arm around me, close, protecting me with his presence. Daddy is so nice and sweet and caring. And... I know he didn't really like the idea of Emily and I coming to this party, but he let us, and then also he showed up to help us when we were in trouble.

I don't know what would have happened otherwise. I don't think it would have been anything too bad, but...

I mean, everything that did happen is a million times better.

The night's over, though. We stand on the sidewalk outside the frat house. It's past midnight at this point, but I don't know exactly what time. I'm getting sleepy, but there's also this gnawing pang of *something* tugging at my core. I can't quite figure out what it is until Daddy slides his fingers over my hip, pushing in a little at the bottom near my hip bone, and then...

Whoosh!

I don't know what just happened but I suddenly want to have a lot of sex. Like... a lot a lot. Daddy and I had sex earlier, though. Except, oh wait! I didn't cum. I want to cum. *I want Daddy to make me cum.*

Now that I'm no longer distracted by the party, my mind realizes it can fully focus on the orgasm I didn't have earlier, and that it definitely wants to have sooner rather than later.

Maybe even right here. I'm tempted. Can I get away with grinding against Daddy's leg in the street? Except Emily's right there. No! I can't do that! I...

"Let's go back to my dorm, Fifi," Emily says, smiling at me. "It's close. We can walk!"

GREY

When tonight first started, this is sort of what I figured would happen. Fiona would go back to Emily's dorm room for the night and then we'd meet up the next morning.

That was before, oh, I don't know... I crashed the frat party they were at? Yeah... that's changed things up in a way I didn't expect. Also that whole "punishment" thing where I made Fiona keep herself at the edge of orgasm for a few minutes just to torment her. Holy shit, that was hot. My cock still aches from the memory of Fiona's tight pussy squeezing hard against my shaft for longer than I thought possible.

I probably would have forgiven her if she came right then and there. Maybe a few swats on the ass when I had her alone again, but nothing too crazy. I don't want her to enjoy her punishments if I can help it, even though I know full well she loves most of what we do together. It's just, uh... yeah...

Look, I don't want her to get caught up in some screwed up auction where she's the prize ready to be won. Or anything even remotely like that. It's not about this specific situation but about her figuring out life and realizing that I can't always be there to protect her. I was there tonight, barely, but what if I wasn't?

I have no idea. We don't have to worry about that right now. Instead, we've got something even worse going on.

Fiona has been giving me her patented "fuck me, Daddy" eyes ever since we got outside. And, look, baby girl, I totally get it. I pushed you to the edge but didn't let you go all the way over, so you must be super fucking horny at this point. It doesn't help that I really couldn't help myself and I felt the need to tease the fuck out of her randomly when we were dancing together.

I don't know, man... the look in her eyes whenever any part of me pressed tight against her core. Plus the fact that I still have her panties in my pocket. And she begged me to cover her in white after I take off her dress later...

I'm ready and willing to do exactly that, except then my sister comes along and asks Fiona if she wants to go back to the dorms with her.

My own sister is inadvertently cockblocking me. Fuck. To be fair, I think I did a good job of cockblocking her, too. Porter, don't do it, man. I'll know. I don't know how I'll know, but I will, and then we're going to have some serious issues, so...

Fiona looks up at me, a little timid and worried, but also with a strange sort of confidence in her eyes.

"Um... what would you say if I went back to Dave's room with him?" she asks Emily.

That's me. I'm Dave for the night. Yes. We're doing this. We can do this.

Except, you know, Emily stares at Fiona like her best friend just told her that the end of days is happening and this is our last night on this planet.

"Oh my gosh," Emily says, keeping her mouth open wide, doing a great job of acting completely scandalized.

Then she laughs, but it's the kind of laugh you hear in a dark room in an insane asylum so this isn't even helping.

"What are you going to do back in his room?" my little sister finally manages to ask.

"I mean, I don't know?" Fiona answers with a shrug. "Stuff?"

They're fully into it at this point and I don't want to be the instigator, so as soon as Fiona lets go of my arm, I take a few steps back and go for a short walk to give them time to sort this out. Because, yeah, I love my sister, but I'm getting really tempted to tell her to shut up and go back to her dorm room so I can fuck the shit out of her best friend.

Which isn't good. That's not going to help anyone. And that's not the way I want to tell Emily that Fiona and I have something going on. That we're dating. That... I mean, they're about to talk about *that* so I'll just let them do it.

"Stuff!" Emily says, like the word is some sort of ancient curse. "Fiona, you can't just say you're going to do stuff! Are you... oh my gosh are you going to lose your virginity?"

And... so technically it's impossible for Fiona to lose her virginity tonight. I helped her out with that one and took hers awhile back, so, uh...

Are we going with technicalities here? I don't know. I'm leaving this up to Fiona.

She decides that it's also impossible for me to take her virginity tonight, or else she straight up lies to her best friend. I know Fiona pretty well and I'm going to go with the former. She hates lying, and I think she hates lying to me or Emily most of all.

"Um, no?" Fiona says, stuck in the middle of her answer. "I mean, nope! Right?"

That last one is directed at me. I look at the two girls standing a few feet away from me having a conversation about losing their virginity right in front of a frat house in the middle of the night. Look, I won't judge, but I think we could all have this conversation in a much classier setting. Or just not have it at all, because Emily's going to stay a virgin forever. Right? I'm her older brother and I was her legal guardian for a long time. I mean, she's eighteen now so I guess she's technically on her own, but I think that's bullshit so I'm just going to say no sex for my sister forever and be done with it.

Emily glares at me, then turns back to Fiona. With Fiona she's bright and cheery. This is bullshit, by the way. I didn't even do anything, Emily! Not yet, at least.

You and Fiona are the ones getting into trouble here. I came and save your asses and this is the thanks I get? Fucking A...

"Go have fun," Emily says to her best friend with a

quick nod. "But don't let him be mean to you or pressure you into anything! Alright?"

Fiona nods, taking this seriously. "Yup, I won't. Promise."

I've never pressured Fiona into anything. And I definitely won't be mean to her. She's going to love every single second of what I have in store for us once we get back to the hotel...

I think we're about to do that, to go back, but then Emily stomps over to me, hands on her hips, glaring up like she's some sort of five-foot-four whirlwind of reckoning. No offense, but my little sister isn't scaring anyone, least of all me. I guess she could scare Porter looking like this, but I doubt he'd be scared so much as confused about what's going on.

Emily growls at me. No fucking joke, she growls. Holy shit. Is this my sister? Yeah...

Good job, though. I like it. If you can't actually be tough, might as well make everyone think you're crazy.

It'd work except I know her too well. She doesn't know that right now, though.

"You listen to me, Dave," Emily says, poking my chest with one finger. "My older brother is here and he'll kick your ass if you try anything with Fiona! *Capiche?*"

Are you fucking serious? *Capiche?* Uh... are you trying to act like you're somehow involved in the mafia? I know people think big businesses probably have mafia connections, but unless there's something I don't know about I'm pretty sure our family has nothing even remotely to do with that.

I mean, I'm the head of the family right now, so I think I would know. Also if we did have mafia connections I don't think anyone would include Emily in them. She's, uh... yeah...

I don't even know. I am having a real hard time keeping my composure right now and not busting out laughing.

I nod, trying to look super serious and grave. Sincere as fuck, that's what I'm going for.

Emily nods back at me, then turns to walk away. This goes well for all of half a second before she spins around and then drags two fingers across her throat like she's threatening my life.

Yeah, alright. I don't roll my eyes, but I want to. I'm going to make fun of her forever after this, too. I'll try not to blow my cover, but I'm going to figure out a way to mock her relentlessly for her weirdo bullshit.

"*Adios, senorita!*" Emily says to Fiona.

Fiona stares at me, then at Emily. She keeps a straight face through most of this, but at the sudden Mexican-Spanish-whatever-the-fuck Emily is doing to intimidate me into behaving, Fiona just can't. She nearly falls onto the sidewalk when she starts laughing. Emily shushes her and tells her to play it cool, keep this guy in line, and I try to go along with it, but...

I don't know. I'm just going to stand here and wait until mý sister goes home? Say nothing, do nothing, be good until Emily is out of sight, and then drag Fiona back to the room where I can give her a beautiful Valentine's Day orgasm. That's what we're calling this right now. It'll be real fucking romantic. Also orgasmic. Like, at least one, but preferably a few. Fourteen orgasms? It's the fourteenth so why not? Have to stick to the numbers and do it right, you know?

Emily and Fiona hug it out and Fiona somehow manages to keep her laughter under control. She squeezes Emily and then scurries over to me, taking her proper place nestled tight under my arm. I hold her close and Emily glares at me, but she smiles a little, too.

Look, I would never hurt Fiona, so...

But she doesn't know that, and the protective part of me really appreciates that Emily wants to look out for her best friend, the girl I fell in love with.

"Bye!" Emily says, waving to us. "Just, um... listen, Fiona... I don't think you should bring Dave or whatever his real name is to breakfast tomorrow. Maybe come find me in the dorms in the morning? I really don't think Daddy would like it. I know you don't always see it, but I swear he's super protective of you, too. Probably even more than he is of me now since I'm at college and that's got to be really rough for him, you know?"

"That's not true," Fiona says, shaking her head quick. "Daddy is definitely super protective of you, Emily. I know you're at college now but he came all this way just to make sure everything was safe for your first college party, so..."

"That's true," Emily says. Grinning, she adds, "I'm surprised he didn't burst into the party and scream our names and then drag us out. Woo girl, we should probably never show him these dresses..."

Yeah. That one's true. So fucking true. What the hell, Emily? Don't go wearing clothes that barely cover your ass at a party full of horny frat bros. Fuck!

I contain myself, though. It's almost over. Almost, except...

Emily leaves, walking back towards the dorms. Porter and his friends are standing down the block so she hurries to catch up with them. I'm sure she's safe, but...

"You want to follow her to make sure she gets back to the dorms alright?" Fiona asks, showcasing her newfound psychic abilities.

Seriously, is she a mind reader or what? I know the college campus and dorm building isn't that far away, but still.

"Yeah," I say with a nod. "If you don't mind? Just want to make sure everything's alright. I mean, she's a brat, but she's my little sister, you know?"

"I'm a brat sometimes, too," Fiona says, smirking at me.

"Yeah, you are, but that's different. I'll deal with your brattiness when we get back to the hotel, baby girl..."

28

FIONA

Daddy and I walk through the quiet hotel lobby. I'm kind of glad it's really late right now. Nobody's here except for a few men manning the front desk, which isn't really a problem but as soon as Daddy and I pass by them they openly gape at me.

Um... so... maybe this dress really is a little too much. I cling even tighter to Daddy, holding his arm as we walk past the front desk to the hallway that goes to the elevators. Daddy shakes his head at me and sighs once we're out of view of the front desk guys.

"See?" he says, grumbling. "I get it, Fiona. That dress is smoking hot and you look like a fucking... well, let's not even start with that one. You look hot, that's it."

"Let's not even start with what one?" I ask, scrunching up my eyebrows.

"No," he says, staying strong.

He pushes the button to call the elevator down to us and I just stand there, pouting at him and clinging to him.

"Please, Daddy? I want to know what you were going to say!"

The elevator comes quickly and we step inside as soon as the doors open. It's still just the two of us, now surrounded by half-mirror walls on three sides. Daddy pushes the button for our floor, then stands there, ignoring me as best he can while waiting for the elevator doors to close.

"*Please...*" I beg, pouting at him.

"I'm pretty sure you just gave those two guys at the front desk the wrong idea," Daddy says, reluctant to speak.

"Because I'm holding your arm?" I ask, confused. "I don't think they'll tell anyone, though. They don't even really know anyone we know except I guess maybe that girl I don't like that checked us in, so it's fine."

"Yeah, uh, that's not what I meant," he says. "Fiona, they probably thought I found a prostitute somewhere and brought her back to my room for some fun. Or we're going to make a porn. You could pass as a porn star right now. I mean that in the best way possible. You're really fucking hot, especially when we aren't stuck in some dim frat house party room surrounded by a ton of people, so..."

"Wait! What? I'm... I'm a porn star?" I ask, extra confused.

"I mean, going to be honest, I hope you aren't considering getting into porn. I'd be so fucking jealous, even if you only did lesbian porn. No way I could handle that."

"What if I did porn with just you?" I ask, teasing him.

"That's... better... maybe... but then I'd get jealous of

guys jerking off to you even if I was the one actually fucking the shit out of you, so I don't think that's going to work."

"What if we make one for ourselves and only we watch it?" I ask him, going the extra mile to play devil's advocate.

It's not like I want to be a porn star. Also, is that why they were gaping at me? They think Daddy bought me for the night? Actually, now that I think about it...

"I kind of am your prostitute if you think about it," I say out loud.

Daddy chokes on air, starts coughing, and stares at me. When he can finally speak again, he says, "What? Uh..."

"You bought me at the frat house, so... I mean, that wasn't really the point, but I guess we can pretend?"

He chuckles and shakes his head at me. "If you want to play games like that sometime, we can," he says. "I want you to be with me because you want to be with me, though. I'm not really into the whole payment plan for sexual favors thing."

I shrug, unsure. It's not that I want to... to sell myself... honestly I didn't even really like being in the auction at first either, except afterwards when I found out Daddy was there and he bought me. It's just... um...

"I think it would be a fun game, that's all," I say. "Just sometimes, maybe. Not just that one, but we can play, like... other games? I pretend to be someone else and you pretend too and we can play like that. Like maybe you're my teacher and I'm your student and I'm being a bad girl in class so you just really have to spank me to get me to be good..."

I nod fast. Yup! I like when Daddy spanks me. It's fun, and also kind of embarrassing because I get super wet for him after. Not as wet as I was for him earlier tonight, but if Daddy ever needs a way to get me wet, um... spank me, please?

Spankings are supposed to be punishments, though. I know that, but it's really hard for me to think of them that way anymore.

"Maybe," he says, smiling at me. "Not out in public, though. I don't want anyone getting the wrong idea."

"And I could get a schoolgirl outfit!" I say, clapping. "Yay!"

"Uh, yeah, I was going with the whole prostitute role-play thing first, but I'd also prefer if you didn't wear a sexy schoolgirl outfit out and about, either."

"What if it's Halloween?" I counter.

"I think you should wear a nun's habit," Daddy says. Interrupting me before I can cut in, he adds, "Not a sexy nun, either. Nuns aren't supposed to be sexy, Fiona. Don't even try it."

"I want to be sexy for you, though," I whine.

"Oh yeah?" he asks, and then the door to our elevator opens on our floor. "Show me..."

29

FIONA

Daddy opens the door to our hotel room and gestures like a gentleman for me to go in first. I step inside into the darkness. He enters behind me and lets go of the door. It slowly shuts, trapping us both in here. We're alone, together, in the dark...

He reaches for the light switch next to me but I touch his hand and shake my head. I don't know if he can see me, though.

"No," I say, soft. "Please. Can we keep the lights off? I want to be sexy for you, Daddy..."

He grins. I can see his teeth flash white in the faint light of the moon shining through our balcony window. My dress shines as it reflects a little glimmer of that light, too. Taking Daddy's hand in mine, I lead him to our bed. Just the one, just for us. Do we ever need two beds?

We have them at home. Daddy has his room and his bed and I have my room and my bed. I'm always in Daddy's bed, though. Even when we aren't doing anything sexy, I like sleeping there. I like being able to smell Daddy on his pillows and his blankets, and I like seeing all of the little things around his room that remind me of him.

Sometimes when he's at work I'll curl up in his bed and take a nap while I cling to his blankets. It's not quite the same as being with Daddy and cuddling with him, but I think it's probably the next best thing. It's cozy and comfortable.

We will *not* be doing cozy and comfortable things in bed right now, though. I mean, unless Daddy's cock thrusting inside of me feels very cozy and comfortable, that is. Which it kind of does now that I think about it, but it also feels like a lot of other things so I don't know if that counts the same.

I let go of Daddy's hand once we're at the foot of the bed. He stands there, smirking at me, waiting for my next move. And my next move is...

I push him onto the bed. He lands on his butt, sitting in front of me. Before he can say or do anything else, I climb onto his lap and straddle him. My panties are in his pocket so there's nothing stopping me from getting direct access to my clit right now.

My poor, sensitive, throbbing clit...

Daddy did that. He teased me so much that my clit's felt much more sensitive for the whole night. I press my palms against Daddy's chest and I push him back until he's laying on the bed with me on top of him. Slow, not wanting to tease myself too much, I grind softly against the front of Daddy's pants.

I can feel him growing bigger and bigger beneath me.

My clit slides up and down his pants-covered shaft. Ohhh, yes, please, Daddy. I just want to...

I slide a little faster, grinding my clit against him, caught up in the sudden realization that Daddy's all mine right now and we can do whatever we want. I can do whatever I want to him. I didn't plan on having an orgasm like this, but now that I've started I kind of think maybe I should finish?

I'm going to. That's my plan. Except right when I think I could cum in a few more seconds, Daddy flips me off of him and onto my back. I flop onto the bed, my hips still bucking up but now I'm just grinding against empty air.

"Daddy!" I whine and whimper at him, giving him my poutiest face ever.

"Shush," he says, whispering into my ear. "I know you wanted to be sexy for me but I need this. I need you. I want you to cum so fucking hard, Fiona..."

I shush, partly because Daddy told me to, and partly because of what he just said. How does he want me to cum? I'm very intrigued and interested and...

Daddy kisses me fast and I start to kiss him back, to make out with him, to let our tongues dance and play together, but as soon as I start he stops. He slides down my body until he's right between my legs. Wrenching my dress up, not even bothering to take it off, he pushes my thighs apart and then buries his face between them.

I let out a sharp gasp. *Ohhhh! Yes, Daddy!*

That would be more than enough to make me cum very very soon, but Daddy has other plans for me. He slides two fingers up and down my slit, coating them in my arousal, and then he pushes them inside me. It's not the same as having Daddy's cock inside me, but it's good in a different way. Especially now, especially because...

Daddy curls his fingers up, taking no prisoners. This is it. I'm done before I've even started. His fingers press firm against my g spot, rough and needy. He thrusts them up and down, hard. Usually Daddy starts out slow when he does this, and then he works his way up to more, but right now I'm already way past worked up. I'm ready to burst, so aroused that I feel a constant ache and greedy desire thrumming through my core.

Daddy licks up and down my clit, no more teasing, doing exactly what he knows I like and doing it in a way that he knows will make me cum quick and hard. His fingers work me like magic, pushing my impending orgasm into me, forcing me higher and higher.

I was so worked up before. I nearly came so many times. But I didn't. Daddy didn't want me to right then. I was being punished because I was kind of a bad girl and Daddy came to save me, and...

No more punishments. This is all for me. This is all pleasure.

Thank you, Daddy...

My hips rock up and down in time with Daddy's thrusting fingers. I can't control myself anymore and my entire body starts to shake. Daddy pins me to the bed with his other hand, keeping my legs spread with the rest of his arm. He licks my clit over and over, relentless, while he fucks me hard with his fingers, a never ending assault on my two most sensitive spots; inside and out.

I cum so hard it hurts, but in the best possible way. The ache spreads through my body and I want to keep aching like this forever. I love being sore after Daddy has his way with me. I love to...

My mind is a mess and I can barely think straight anymore. I'm glad we're laying on the bed because I don't think I can walk or move, either. My body tingles and I can still feel Daddy's fingers inside me, but he's not trying to make me cum anymore. He's just playing with me and touching me. It feels nice, but it's not the same. This is soft and soothing and sweet.

He slides up alongside me, fingers still in my pussy, and he kisses me gently on the cheek.

"Thank you, Daddy," I say, kissing him back. I just kind of kiss the air next to his cheek because I'm having a hard time focusing right now.

"You're welcome, baby girl," Daddy says, moving into my kiss and making it easier for me. "You look tired. You want to go to bed now?"

"I'm a little sleepy..." I mumble to him.

"Does that mean you're going to fall asleep on me?" he asks, smirking. "Because I was planning on making you cum again and if I remember correctly you mentioned something about covering you in white after I got you out of this dress, so..."

"Nope! I'm awake! No sleeping!" I say, snapping my eyes open. I sit up, or I try to, but I only manage to get halfway before toppling back to the bed.

Daddy laughs. "You want to try out the whirlpool? We

can relax in there for a few with the lights down low. I think that'd be nice."

"What about sex, though?" I ask, because this is a sticking point for me. "Can we have sex in there?"

"Whoa, calm yourself," he says with a grin. "You can barely even sit up. I'll go start the water and help you out of your dress and then we'll see what we can do. Alright?"

"Alright," I say, smiling wide. "Thank you so much, Daddy."

GREY

How fucking lucky am I? Seriously, I ask myself that question every day and I still haven't figured out the answer.

I never really thought I'd ever be with Fiona. It's not something that was on my radar until the one day that we just so happened to give in to each other and we made it work. Sort of. I'm not sure if it's actually working or if I'm hoping and praying that everything continues to go smoothly.

And... yeah, so the brat teased the fuck out of me and there was a lot going on that day, but still. I could have stopped it, or tried harder. Maybe I should have. I'm still not sure what the fuck I'm doing or if this is a good move or a terrible one.

Right now none of that matters, though. What matters is I have the most beautiful, perfect, amazing, sexy, cute, fun, wonderful... all of it. Every fucking adjective you can think of that's good, that's what Fiona is to me. And I want to make sure I'm all of the good ones to her, too.

While she lays on the bed in our hotel room, I slip away to the bathroom and turn on the lights. I twist the dimmer to keep the lights low and nice, because ambiance and romance isn't lost on me.

Look, I get that I teased the fuck out of her in the frat house when I had her alone for seven minutes, but I still want to be romantic with this girl. It's not just about giving her amazing orgasms and sexual fulfillment. Fiona fulfills me in so many ways and I want to do the same for her. I...

Enough about me. We're done with that. I struggle with it every day and half the time I think this is all some sort of fucked up joke and I'll wake up and she'll realize that I'm twelve years older than her and that maybe she'd be better off with a younger guy. That hasn't happened yet and I don't want it to ever happen, but if it does, uh...

I don't know what I'll do. I'll figure it out if it happens.

I twist the hot water knob in the whirlpool tub. Then back and forth, gradually turning the hot and the cold knobs until the water coming out of the faucet is just right. Warmer than warm, but not too hot. The perfect temperature to relax and unwind after an eventful day.

Just as I'm about to go back into the bedroom and carry her in here, I spot a neat little bottle of lavender scented bubble bath on the bathroom counter. Was that here before? Who the fuck knows? It looks perfect for the occasion at hand, though. I grab it, unscrew the top, and pour it in with the spray from the faucet. Bubbles rise up immediately, sweet and flowery.

Shit, this is amazing. I should get some of this for back home, just drag Fiona into the bath so we can soak in the bubbles and water. Seems perfect to me.

I leave the tub to do its thing, fill up, whatever, and I head back into the bedroom. Fiona lays there, curled up on her side, dress still hiked up to her waist. I take a moment to glance with supreme appreciation at the glorious ass on this girl. Yoga has fine tuned her body into a perfectly curved masterpiece and I'm more than happy to show her exactly how much I appreciate it all the time.

My cock throbs in my pants, begging to spring out and sink deep inside her as soon as possible. Not yet, though. I have no fucking clue if we'll end up doing that at all considering she could barely stay awake a few minutes ago. Maybe later, but right now it's about Fiona and I want to take care of her and be everything to her. She calls me "Daddy," but it's not just some kinky sex thing or a funny nickname that she started using because of a joke with my sister. It's not just that anymore, at least. "Daddy" means a lot to both of us. It means she's my baby girl and I'm going to do everything in my power to take care of her, and it means I'm her protector and I need to keep her safe no matter what.

And, you know, sometimes that involves spankings or orgasm denial, or any other number of interesting punishments because Fiona isn't always the pure and innocent good girl that she looks like on the outside. Sometimes she's naughty, sometimes it's on purpose, sometimes she's a brat, and...

I don't know if I should admit this, but I like all facets

of Fiona. If she was too bratty all the time that'd be frustrating, but she's just bratty enough to really get me going, and after she's a perfect little angel. She does a few naughty things, but she knows where the line is and she never crosses it. She tries so fucking hard to be a better person even if she doesn't always know how to get there. That's where I come in. I help her when she isn't sure what to do.

Honestly she's amazing and it frustrates the fuck out of me that her mother doesn't realize it. That's an entirely separate story, though. I don't want to get into it right now.

I quietly walk towards the side of the bed. Fiona half opens her eyes when I bend over to wake her. I caress her cheek softly and she lets out a cute little sigh before nuzzling against my palm.

"We need to get you out of that dress, baby girl," I tell her.

She mumbles something, a bunch of made up words that don't make sense. I understand her, though. She wants me to do it for her, to help her, to take care of her.

I reach behind her to unzip her dress. And, yeah, this dress is way too much. Everything comes undone as soon as I pull the zipper all the way down. I shift her around, tugging the dress up her body. She moves with me, lifting her butt and arching her back to help me get her naked.

I love her so much. Yes, she's naked in front of me, and my cock wants nothing more than to fuck the shit out of her, but to me this girl is also a prime piece of art. She looks like some sort of classical art model, moonlight shining on her body and highlighting everything amazing about her. I kind of want to take a picture of her like this, blow it up, frame it, and hang it in my home office.

Tousled, messed up hair curls over her face like a sleepy little blanket. Fiona stretches her arms up above her head and yawns. I watch her chest as she shudders away her sleepiness. Her entire body shakes, curves bouncing in the most delicious way, and then everything settles back down once she's done.

It's like sexy magic or something. Seriously, holy fucking shit. This girl does way too much to me. I can't take it. I want every memory with her, every picture I have of her in my mind, to last forever.

"What about you, Daddy?" she asks, cute and soft, looking over at me.

I'm still dressed, just standing at the side of the bed, admiring her.

I smile and start to take off my clothes, slow and easy. She watches me, intent, a faint blush creeping across her cheeks. She always gets a little shy and nervous whenever we get naked together, even though we've spent more time than I ever could have imagined being naked together.

Even when we're back home and we fall asleep, when I hold Fiona tight in my arms as she cuddles against me, sometimes I wake up to her blushing and mumbling to herself as she realizes we just slept naked together the entire night.

It's amazing. Seriously, I'm the luckiest man alive.

I let the cloak I borrowed fall to the floor. I guess I'll have to figure out a way to return that later. No clue how, but I can't say it's a huge priority at the moment. My suit jacket and dress shirt come next. Fiona's lips slip open a little wider with each button I undo until she's staring at me with an "O" face. I slip off my shirt and let it fall to the floor, acting like she doesn't turn me on as much as she does.

She's about to see just exactly what she does to me, though. I can't hide it for much longer.

I kick my shoes off. Fiona licks her lips slowly when I start to undo my pants. I think we're both incredibly aware of the bulge I'm sporting right now. I peel my khaki pants and my boxer briefs down at the same time. As soon as I get them lowered to mid-thigh, my cock bounces up, hard and ready for whatever life has to offer it.

Careful, tentative, Fiona reaches out to lightly wrap her fingers around my shaft while I remove my pants and underwear. I let her do what she wants, but I try not to act too excited about it. I mean, this girl makes me feel like a fucking sex-crazed teenager constantly, but I like to pretend I have a little more self-control than that. She strokes me, her mouth still open, lips parted, while I stand there in the buff.

"Daddy," she says, giggling quietly. "You're hard."

"Oh yeah?" I ask, acting like I've only just realized it.

"Uh huh..." she murmurs, eyes never leaving my cock.

"I thought we were taking a bath," I tell her. "You sure woke up fast."

"Nooooo, I'm sleepy," she mumbles, pretending to yawn. "See?"

"Sleepy and stroking my cock like you never want to let go."

"It's mine," she says with a nod. "For me."

It is. It's only for her. Only when she's a good girl, though. And she's been a very good girl ever since I came and saved her from being auctioned off to some random dude at the Sigma Epsilon Chi frat house, so...

We'll see what happens. She might crash on me once I get her to the tub. If so, I guess I'm fucked, and not in the way I prefer.

"Come here you brat," I say, ignoring her hand on my cock as I scoop her up in my arms.

She pouts and whines a little, letting go of me, but as soon as I have her cradled close to my chest she lets out a cute little sigh and nuzzles against me. I carry her like that to the bathroom where I have the lights dimmed and the water still running. The tub is nearly overflowing now, bubbles barely contained.

Fiona giggles at the sight of the bubbles, somehow looking beautifully innocent despite the fact that we're both completely naked and I have a raging hard-on throbbing somewhere in the vicinity of her perfectly curvy ass.

"Bubbles!" she says, looking from the tub to me. "They smell nice. It's lavender?"

"Yeah," I say, smiling down at her. "I thought you'd like it."

"I love it. Thank you, Daddy." Then she yawns, slow and languorous. "Lavender makes me sleepy, though."

"Good. You need to rest. Today's been a long day."

"Yup, but it was a lot of fun," she says with a sleepy little nod. "I'm tired but I don't want to fall asleep on you when, um... you have *that*..."

She tilts her head to the side and tries to look down at my cock. I ignore her, because this isn't about me right now. Careful, I brace myself and lean over the edge of the tub, gently lowering her into the water.

A shiver runs through her body as she sinks into the hot bubble bath. I slide her up against one side so she can sit on her own, and then I step in with her, my cock bouncing comically every throbbing inch of the way. She stares, eyes glued to my obvious arousal, until I sink into the bubbles with her.

"This is nice," she says, smiling, eyes half-closed. "We should take bubble baths more often."

"The tub at home is a little small, but I've always thought an outdoor hot tub would be nice," I say.

"Oooh... in the backyard?"

"Yeah, what do you think? I know a guy who can do it. Lots of times people get them installed on the back porch, but I think a small gazebo type of deal would be nicer. Enclosed for a little extra privacy."

"I like privacy when I'm with you, Daddy..." Fiona says, eyes gleaming in the most sinfully seductive way possible.

Yeah, I'm done. I don't know what the fuck is going to happen, but she's caught me in whatever spell she wants me in and I can't get away even if I try.

"If we had a hot tub in the backyard with privacy like that, then..." she says, each word slow and teasing. "...we could close the doors, and... wait, would it have doors?"

"Yeah, like frosted glass doors," I say as she slides across the tub to my side.

"What about a light?" she asks, lifting herself up and crawling into my lap. "Or curtains? Would anyone be able to see us in there?"

"I'm sure we could figure that one out," I say, letting her do what she wants, my hands resting on her hips.

"I just really want a lot of privacy, Daddy," Fiona pouts. "Because then we could do... *this*..."

She reaches behind her, hand disappearing beneath the bubbles. Her fingers search under the water for my throbbing cock. Stroking me a couple of times, she finishes with her fingers down at the base of my shaft, and then she lowers herself further into the water. She guides me towards her as she sinks down deep. My cock finds the most amazing spot, lodging right between her slick lips, and as soon as she has me trapped she pushes all the way down until I'm deep inside her.

"Fuck!" I gasp, unable to come up with any other word than that.

I need this.

I need her.

I always will.

31

FIONA

W hen I sink down onto Daddy's cock and he lets out a sharp gasp and says "Fuck!" that's when I know I'm a very good girl right now. His hands grip the tub, fingers pressed hard against the side. I slowly lift up until Daddy's cock is almost about to pop out of me, and then I slide back down again.

I stay down this time, holding him inside me. I reach for his cheeks and I frame his face with my palms. Sweet, like Daddy's little angel, I lean in and kiss his lips. Soft little kisses, over and over again. Our lips touch, and then I kiss up to his nose, to the side, I kiss each of his cheeks, and I end with my lips pressed against the stubble on his chin. It tickles a little and makes me smile.

"Daddy?" I ask, feeling all of him inside me. "I'm your good girl, right?"

He nods, his breath fast, hitched. "Yes, baby. Always."

"Nope, not always," I say, pouting a little. "I'm sorry, Daddy. I'll try to be good all the time, alright?"

He nods and his eyes open a little as he smiles at me. "I know you will," he says.

I slide up and down Daddy's cock again, the warmth of the water and the bubbles closing in on us like a sweet smelling blanket. Lavender makes me sleepy, but riding up and down on Daddy's cock excites me. I'm trapped in the middle, half in a daze and half excited beyond belief.

I came earlier, though. Daddy teased me all through the night, but then he gave me a really big orgasm after. It was amazing. I don't know if I would want to do that all the time. I don't think I could handle it all the time! But every so often... especially if I'm not being as good of a good girl as I really should be, well...

That's a good reminder for why I should be good. I'm glad that Daddy thought I was good enough at the end of the night to deserve a wonderful orgasm like the one he gave me.

But now I want to give Daddy an orgasm, too. I want him to cum inside me again like he did before. I want him to relax in the bath and let me ride his cock and then we can cuddle in the bubbles and... and... and...

I love Daddy so much. I want to be with him forever, all the time, and always.

I need you, Daddy...

"Daddy?" I ask him. "Can we turn on the jets for the whirlpool stuff?"

He smiles at me. Without answering, he reaches over to the console near the faucet and pushes a button. The whirlpool tub jets surge to life. Insistent streams of water crash against our bodies. I'm on one side of the tub with

Daddy, but even the jets behind me feel nice. One of them presses gently against the side of my butt, while another sprays into my hip and the side of my thigh.

Daddy shifts a little to the side. I think he enjoys the feeling of the water against his back, which is what I wanted when I asked him if we could turn the jets on. I want Daddy to feel nice and relaxed and happy and then I want Daddy to cum, and...

This is my plan, except when Daddy moves to the side, one of the jets behind him comes shooting towards me. I don't really know how all of the angles and that stuff works, I just know what I feel, and what I'm feeling right now is, um...

The water shooting out of the whirlpool jet presses hard against my clit. I lean back, caught off guard by the rapid sensation. Daddy watches me, alarmed at first, eyes wide, but then I think he realizes what's going on and he grins.

He grabs my hips, holding me tight. His arm blocks the jet against my clit for a second, but then he moves his elbow up, letting the swirl resume and overtake me.

"I... oh my..." I mumble.

This... this is supposed to be about Daddy, about making him cum, and... I'm not... um...

I'm not going to cum *right* now, but if this keeps up I make no promises about what the future may hold.

I grind against Daddy's cock, which also kind of ends up being me grinding against the jet stream from the whirlpool tub. I don't know if you can grind against water, but my body sure does want to give it a good try. My pussy clenches against Daddy's shaft, the spray of water sending spasms through my entire body.

The introduction of these whirlpool jets also has one unintended side effect. The bubbles from the bubble bath start growing and growing. They multiply, rise up to our shoulders, and then even more until we're trapped in a cloud of bubbles. I'm not sure Daddy or I care about that, though. We move and writhe and enjoy each other's bodies and the feeling of our souls touching as we make love in the steamy, hot water.

Now it's just us. Bubbles circle us on all sides, with only the space between us clear enough that we can see each other. We might as well be in some fantasy cloud world because I can't see anything besides bubbles and Daddy. I can't feel anything besides the warm water and Daddy's cock inside me and his hands on my hip. Oh, and the whirlpool jet streaming against my clit. That last one's kind of important, too.

"Daddy, I... I think I..." I mumble, trying to find words.

"You can," he tells me, reassurance and soft sweetness in his voice. I love when Daddy is sweet to me. "You can cum again for me, baby girl. I'm going to cum, too. Don't worry."

"I like that," I tell him, smiling before closing my eyes and enjoying every second of ecstasy. "I like when you cum, Daddy. I like when I make you cum."

"You turn me on so fucking much," he says, voice rough, groaning. "It's almost impossible not to cum when I'm with you, Fiona."

"Good," I say, kissing him gently on the lips. "That's

why we're good together, Daddy. I'm always like that with you, too. Even when I think I can't cum anymore, um... welp, you seem to find a new way to make me do it, so..."

He smirks at me and kisses me back, lips lingering against mine.

"I love you," he says. "So much. I can't ever stop loving you."

"I love you, too," I tell him. "I love you a lot, Daddy. I don't want to ever stop loving you, so can we just love each other forever?"

"Yes," he says with a grin.

"Yay," I say, grinning right back at him.

The whirlpool jet is taking its toll on me. The insistent, greedy water surges against my clit creating a need and a desire I didn't realize was possible. I mean, the fact of the matter is that I didn't know I could have as strong an orgasm as I had on the hotel bed a little while earlier, but Daddy made that one possible. I like to cum, and I like to cum as many times as I can, but sometimes I just feel all, um... cummed out? Is that a thing?

But, nope, definitely going to cum again with this jet and Daddy's cock inside me. Very very soon, too...

I grind and squeeze and clench against Daddy's cock. He holds my hips and guides me in the water. Daddy doesn't play fair all the time, but that's alright. I like how he has so many surprises for me. I've learned so much about myself and my body while I'm with Daddy. Sometimes it's sexy, like right now, but other times it's just useful stuff like how to apply for jobs or what to say at interviews.

The two are very separate! No sexy interviews for me. Unless I applied for a job at Daddy's company as his secretary, and then maybe I'd try to convince him a sexy interview would be fun. This is also why I haven't done that, because I know Daddy has to work and I would distract him all day on accident and he'd never get anything finished.

Weekends are good times for distractions, though. Or the morning. Or at night. Really any time when Daddy doesn't have to work, that's a great time for a distraction. I like our current distraction, too.

Lost in bubbles, pinned onto Daddy's cock by his firm grip, the jet of the whirlpool spraying hard against my clit, I lose myself in the moment, the feeling, the love and wonder, the... the *everything*...

My legs clamp down hard, squeezing Daddy tight between them. I feel the inside of my thighs snugly wrapped against the outside of his. My body shakes a little and my pussy spasms, mini pulses of pleasure gripping Daddy's shaft. He twitches and trembles inside me. I feel like I'm cumming right here and now, except I also feel like I haven't started yet, too.

It's... it's strange and amazing all at once.

I keep going, a rush of wonder sending quick little spasms all throughout my body. I can feel Daddy throbbing inside me, too. I think he's about to cum, but neither of us has fully cum yet. Our orgasms are imminent, on the edge of becoming a reality, but we're stuck here in the moment right before when the intense ecstasy is so extreme that it feels like your entire body is about to explode with pleasure.

Over. And over. And over.

More, more, more...

My mouth opens and I want to scream but the sound sticks in my throat as if it's waiting for my full orgasm to crash through me before it can come into being. My pussy clenches tighter and tighter around Daddy's cock. I don't know if I can squeeze him any harder, but my body really wants to. Daddy's cock is like one constant pulse right now. I can feel him throbbing inside me, but I can feel throbbing inside of his throbbing.

Everything... everything is... it's so...

A flash of euphoria caresses my body from the inside out. Every muscle I have tightens, impossibly taut. Daddy's cock jerks and thrashes inside me as he fills me with his cum. The only thought I can think right now is that somehow I really did just become an angel filled with pure and perfect plea-sure and I'm Daddy's. He's mine and I'm his and we're covered in bubbles and ecstasy and orgasms and cum and...

Maybe I black out for a little while because I don't even remember what happens after that. I wake up in Daddy's arms and it seems like hours later, but maybe just a few seconds or a minute or who knows how long.

I hug Daddy tight and his cock is still impossibly hard inside me. I feel him throb and twitch, the aftershock of his orgasm tremoring inside me. My pussy instinctively squeezes back against him, tiny jolts of pleasure echoing through us.

Daddy squeezes me tight and holds me in his arms and we just stay like that for a long time, neither of us wanting to let the other go.

"Daddy, I love you so much," I whisper in his ear.

"I love you, too, Fiona," he says, whispering back to me, kissing my earlobe. "So much. So so much."

Our moment of pleasure overload delirium has to end sometime, and eventually it does. Which, um... at that point we realize there's way too many bubbles in the tub.

Both of us look around, kind of in a daze, confused as to how this happened. I start giggling uncontrollably and Daddy laughs, too. Then he shakes his head and smacks my butt under the water. I wiggle in his lap, squeezing against his cock to tease him. He's a little softer now, but I don't care. I just like having Daddy inside me all the time no matter what.

"You made a lot of bubbles," I tell him, matter-of-fact.

"Yeah, well, you're the one who wanted me to turn the whirlpool jets on."

"Oooh, Daddy, I really like the jets," I add, excited.

"Yeah, I could tell," he says with a smirk. "So you want me to look into getting a hot tub for the backyard?"

"Yes please?" I ask, sweet and innocent like a very good girl.

"That might be incredibly dangerous," he adds. "I feel like I'm going to want to drag you into the hot tub every chance I get."

"You can!" I say with a quick nod. "Only if I'm a good girl, though. But I'll be really good, Daddy. Maybe, um...

I'm going to get a job and I want to save up for college, but I can help pay for the hot tub?"

"Fiona..." Daddy says, shaking his head softly. "You don't have to do that. Save your money. I know you want to go to college and make something of yourself. That's a lot more important than a hot tub."

"I just don't like that you'd be buying the hot tub just because we both like being in it together," I say, pouty.

"We can figure it out," he says. "I kind of understand. I don't want you to feel like I'm doing it just for you, but... yeah, I feel like my main consideration at the moment is because of what just happened."

"Also probably we shouldn't put bubbles in the hot tub if you get one," I say, looking all around.

"Seriously, what's with all the bubbles?" he asks. "Holy shit, we're going to fill the whole hotel suite or something."

"Maybe we should turn off the jets?" I offer.

Daddy reaches out to where he thinks the console controls should be. Eventually he finds them after swiping away the bubbles so he can actually see what he's doing, and then he pushes the button to turn the jets off. The whirlpool spray stops, but the bubbles remain.

"Ummmm?" I murmur, looking all around.

"I mean, they've got to go away sometime, right?" Daddy says with a shrug.

"Hopefully!"

"Yeah, uh... let's drain the water and get out and see how that goes."

"What if we got sent to another world by bubble magic and we're trapped there?" I ask.

"Well, that would kind of suck and I think Emily would be pissed about both of us vanishing without a trace," Daddy says.

"Oh no... I didn't think of that," I say, frowning.

"Hey, no frowning," he says.

"I don't want Emily to be sad, though."

"Yeah, well, what are you going to tell her about going back to Dave's room..." Daddy says with a grin. "She might be sad after that."

"Um... maybe... I... I don't know? I'll tell her Dave is nice but then I just came back here because I missed you, Daddy. What if I tell her that?"

"How about we tell her the truth soon?" Daddy asks.

"Is that alright?" I counter. "I know, um... it's hard, because... I don't want Emily to be mad at you or me or anyone, really."

"I know," he says. "I think she'll understand, though. We'll figure it out, alright?"

"Alright," I say, sneaking in to kiss him quick. "I don't want Emily to be sad but I'm excited to tell her."

"Just, uh... don't tell her everything, alright? Like... I don't know about the girl talk you two do together, but I think we should probably keep the details of our sex life private."

I nod fast. "Um, yes. No telling Emily that you spank me."

"I mean, yeah, that one is a good start. I was thinking, you know, all of it, though."

230

"No telling Emily that you made me play with myself until I could barely stand it and wouldn't let me cum at the frat party?"

Daddy stares at me while I try to keep a straight face. I can't hold it for very long, though. I burst into a silly grin and no matter how hard I try I just can't stop smiling.

"Yeah, now you're just fucking with me," he says, grinning back at me. "Cut it out, brat."

"Noooo, I'm just teasing you!" I say. "I wouldn't tell Emily any of that. That would be weird. I'll just tell her that you love me and I love you and we're perfect together."

"Sounds good," Daddy says, laughing a little. "I think I'll tell her the exact same thing."

GREY

Fiona and I deal with the bubbles. This is going to be one of those don't ask don't tell situations. The bubbles have been exterminated. That's all you need to know.

Also, Fiona looks so fucking hot waltzing around naked and shiny, fresh out of the tub. Maybe it's the bubbles. I don't fucking know. I just know that even though we just had amazing orgasms together, I kind of want to toss her on the bed, pin her arms above her head, and rail the fuck out of her until I literally can't move anymore.

I can't do that right now. I want to, but it's physically impossible. The mind is willing but the body is weak. See what you do to me, Fiona? Ugh.

And then, well...

"Daddy!" Fiona squeals, opening the closet door just outside of the bathroom. "Look. It's bathrobes!"

Sure enough, two fluffy white bathrobes draped across

hangers hang in the closet. She takes one and tries it on, but it's way too small for her. Even still, she wears it. She pulls the sleeves up as best she can so she can tie the little bathrobe belt around her waist. The whole thing makes her look like she's somehow shrunk a couple of sizes, but once she's done she looks happy with the results.

"You too," she says, pulling up the sleeves again so that her hands can reach out and grab the other bathrobe.

She tugs it off the hanger and then scurries over to me. I try to take it from her, but she makes the cutest angry sound ever, kind of an "nnnnfffhhhh," and then she jumps behind me and starts to put the bathrobe on for me. I slide my arms in each of the sleeves, pulling it closed.

I don't even try to tie it off in the front. Fiona hops back in front of me, pulls up her sleeves again even though it barely helps and they fall back over her hands immediately, and somehow manages to grab either end of the fluffy bathrobe belt. She ties it off as best she can, making a bunch of murmurs and nods and all-around looking very focused and intent on what she's doing.

"Good?" I ask her once she's done.

"Your bathrobe fits better," she grumps.

"I'm pretty sure they're the same size," I tell her.

"My sleeves are too big, though," she pouts.

I snicker, and she just pouts some more.

"Hold out your hands," I say.

She does, all while watching me, curious. I go for one sleeve first, rolling up the cuff until we finally get it so that her hand is mostly sticking out, visible. She beams at me like I've just performed some sort of witchcraft or wizardry, and then she waves around her other sleeve-covered hand for me to do. I roll up that one too, and then she's mostly good to go.

Mostly. The bathrobe is still comically large on her. She basically disappears inside it. Fiona's got the curves of a goddess but with this bathrobe on she's just a little ball of fluff. She's *my* little ball of fluff, though, so basically I couldn't care less if I can't see her beautifully spankable ass right now.

"I feel like an abominable snowman," she says, then she holds up her hands in what I think is supposed to be a monster pose. "*Rawr!*"

"Yeah, you look like one, too," I say, keeping a straight face.

"Hey!" she shouts, smacking my arm. "Be nice to me, Daddy!"

"I am nice to you. You're the one who roared at me."

"No. I *rawred*. It's different."

"Rawr?"

"Roar is scary, but rawr is cute," she adds.

"So you're a cute little abominable snowman?"

She nods a lot, very fast. "Uh huh!"

"Come here and let me cuddle the fuck out of you then."

"Alright!"

Which, you know, I do. Never going to pass up a chance to cuddle the fuck out of Fiona. Seriously, why would I do that? She's basically the cuddliest person I've ever met. Just cuddles all the fucking time. I'll be in the kitchen trying to make dinner and then all of a sudden I

MIA CLARK

get cuddled. I'm in the shower, completely unsuspecting, and from out of nowhere comes a naked cuddlebug behind me, wrapping her arms around me.

Fiona is cuddly as fuck in every way possible.

"Sleepytime," she says, hugging me tight and looking up at me.

"You're finally tired?" I ask her. "I figured we'd stay up for a few more rounds, really dig into it, get everything out of our systems."

Her eyes grow wide as she looks up at me, first shocked, then trying to figure out if I'm serious or not, and finally she gets suspicious. She harrumphs at me before quickly shoving her hand in my bathrobe and going straight for my cock.

"Liar!" she says, finding my not-quite-soft but nowhere near hard cock.

"Hey, if you keep that up I won't be a liar for very long..." I say to her.

She strokes me to test if I'm telling the truth. I get a little harder, and I think I could go all the way if she seriously wants to keep it up, but eventually she just shrugs and goes back to hugging me.

"Can we have a night when we get back where we just have sex a million times?" she asks me. "Not tonight, though. I really am sleepy, Daddy. I was just teasing you. You were teasing too, right?"

"Yeah," I say, smiling and kissing the top of your head. "Just teasing you."

"What about the night when we get back where we have sex a million times?"

"I don't know about a million..." I say.

"Nope! It has to be a million!"

"What about, like... ten times?"

"Ten million?"

"What if we track everything and just go for a million as a lifetime goal?"

"Um, can we?" she asks, suddenly excited at the prospect.

"Yeah, sure, why not?"

"Alright!"

Seriously I don't know what the fuck I did to deserve a girl like Fiona but I'm going to make sure I keep doing it for my entire fucking life. A million times and more than that. Fuck, man...

"Daddy?" she asks, nuzzling against me. She says more, but it comes out muffled with her mouth hard against my bathrobe.

"What's that?" I ask, patting her head softly.

"I said, um... can we get blankets and cuddle up outside and look at the stars?"

"You're not going to fall asleep outside on me, are you?" I ask her, one brow raised.

"I'll try to stay awake but if I fall asleep you'll carry me to bed?"

"I suppose I could do that..." I say, hiding a grin.

"Yay," she says, both excited and growing more tired by the second.

We go about stealing the blankets from the bed and then bringing them over to our private balcony. I don't think the balcony was made for blanket stargazing, but who cares? We're doing it. Fiona pulls a pair of patio chairs together for us to sit on, and then we kind of fold the blankets over the chairs. I sit in one, regular, and she sits in the other, with her feet curled up under her while she leans onto my shoulder and holds my arm tight.

I wrap the blankets snug around us, warding off the chill of the night air. It's fucking February and it's kind of cold out. Really not sure stargazing in bathrobes with blankets is a great idea, but Fiona and I make it work.

It's not that cold, either. We've got plenty of warmth to go around. My little fucking cuddlebug over here makes sure of that one. Somehow she knows exactly how to maximize our body heat and make sure that we both stay optimally warm despite being on a balcony during a chilly February night.

And then we stargaze. Fiona looks at all the stars, silent, her eyes flashing this way and that, almost like she's in awe that something like this exists. The night sky is nicer here in Emily's college town and we can see a lot more stars than we can back home. The way she's looking at the sky makes me want to drive her way up north sometime, to a cabin in the middle of nowhere, so we can see all of the stars without any light pollution whatsoever.

I just cuddle with her and look at the stars, too. I recognize some constellations from when I was little. Before the tragic accident with my parents, my dad and I used to do overnight fishing trips and we'd look at the stars while cooking our day's catch over a fire.

I start to point one out to Fiona, but when I look down her eyes are closed. She breathes gently, clinging softly to me. Yeah... you didn't even try, Fiona! Just fell asleep on me after a few minutes. Wow. Way to go.

Nah, it's cool. I like watching her sleep. I love everything about her, and this is just one more thing I get to enjoy.

I stay outside for a little longer. I don't know how long. I look at the stars and I think about things I haven't thought of in a long time. I think about looking at these same stars when Fiona and I are old enough that twelve years doesn't even seem like that much of an age difference anymore.

Eventually I get up. I carefully slide her away from me, doing my best to make sure she doesn't wake up. I stand and scoop her out of the patio chair, blankets and all, and then I carry her back inside. We left a bedside lamp on, but that's it. More than enough light to guide me to bed and tuck her in.

Steady, slow, I get her nestled on the bed and I fix the blankets so she's cuddled up and warm. I go to my side, switch off the lamp, and get in bed under the blankets with her. As soon as we're together again, she lets out a soft yawn and mumbles something, then she crawls under the blankets and latches onto me.

I hold her tight, wrapping her in my arms, and we fall asleep together.

I love her so fucking much.

FIONA

I'm sleepy and I'm cuddling with Daddy and there's music playing but I don't know why. I ignore it and cuddle closer with Daddy, hiding my face against his chest. The music stops eventually, but then a bunch of... I don't know, are those wind chimes? The chimes keep striking, one after another, and then the music starts again, and...

Oh no. Oh no oh no oh no!

That's... that's my phone. And that's my ringtone for when Emily calls me. I don't have a special tone for when she texts me, so the chime is just my regular text one.

Judging by how this is going so far, it seems like she's been texting me a few times, then calling me, then texting me, and... yup, I'm screwed.

"Fiona," Daddy says, grumbling himself awake. "I love you, but seriously, what the fuck is up with your phone?"

"Um, so..." I murmur, trying to hide my voice with a whisper. "That's... Emily?"

"Alright," he says, vaguely accepting this. "Why the fuck is she calling and texting you so much? I don't--"

And then I think it dawns on both of us. I mean, it kind of dawned on me when I first realized that the music wasn't part of a dream or anything, and the wind chimes weren't wind chimes. I just really don't want to be in this situation right now because I don't know how I'm supposed to handle it.

Or how we're going to handle it? Is this my problem to deal with or is Daddy going to help me? I feel like it's mine and mine alone, but I haven't read the text messages or listened to my voicemail yet. I should probably do that.

Reluctant, I slip away from Daddy's side. It's cold without him. I like how warm I feel when I cuddle with Daddy. It's cozy. You can't cuddle on your own, you know? It's just not the same.

I find my phone, which somehow ended up on the floor. I don't remember putting it there, but to be fair I don't really remember putting it anywhere. I'm very good at misplacing my phone. Thankfully Daddy always helps me find it by calling it for me. Yay!

Except I don't need help this time because Emily keeps trying to contact me. Ring ring ring, chime chime chime. Ugh. Calm down, Emily! I'm... I'm getting it, I'm reading, I'm...

I cuddle back up with Daddy before I do my duty as Emily's best friend and read all of her crazy frantic text messages. Daddy yawns and presses his cheek against my forehead, reading with me.

"Fifi, are you awake? Get up. We need to talk. Are you with Dave?"

"Wait, Dave isn't even his real name, right? What's his name?"

"Did you have sex? What's it like? Is it like using a vibrator? What's using a vibrator like? I don't know why you would know. Do you know? I don't know. Do you think I can secretly buy one using Daddy's credit card? I know it's supposed to be for emergencies. Is being really horny and wanting to know what a vibrator feels like an emergency? Text me."

Mostly normal so far. Except the last part. I mean, to be honest, the last part is normal for us, too. I just don't usually read texts like that from her with Daddy looking over my shoulder, so...

I tilt my head to the side and give him the most innocent, cute little look I can muster.

"I love you, Daddy?" I say, as sweet as possible.

"Yeah, I love you, too, but if I find out that Emily has a vibrator that she bought using my credit card..." he says, trailing off. I don't really think he has to finish his thoughts, though.

"So it's fine if she gets one but you don't find out?" I ask, hiding a silly grin.

"I mean, I guess," he grumbles. "Look, I get that, uh...

you girls have needs or whatever the fuck, and I'd rather she deal with those with a vibrator, but I don't want to hear about it."

"What about me?" I ask, sweet and innocent and cute, biting my bottom lip for him. "Will you get a vibrator with me and use it on me and..."

Judging by the way Daddy's cock immediately hardens and presses against my hip, I'm going to say that's a yes. Woo hoo, success!

"Don't be a brat," he says, ignoring his erection.

"Sorry, Daddy!"

And... let's take a break from text messages. How about voicemail messages? Those are always fun. Or I'm going to seriously regret this.

I hit the button for my voicemail and then tap the speakerphone button. I have three new messages. They're all from Emily. Alright, I've got this! I can do it. I...

"Fiona! It's me. Emily. Your best friend. Don't know if you forgot that, but... why are you ignoring my text messages? Wake up! Wake up wake up wake up! Alright, bye."

Followed immediately by:

"Fiona... Emily again. Still your best friend. What are you doing? Are you waking Dave up with a blowjob?

That's still sex, you know? So if you try to tell me later that you didn't have sex with him, but then I find out that you gave him a blowjob... nope, that's sex. What do penises taste like?"

Well, Emily, I only have experience with one penis, but I have *a lot* of experience with that one penis, so...

Daddy's cock tastes nice. It's more the smooth feeling of him in my mouth as I slide my tongue around his shaft and the head of his cock that I like, but when he gets really excited his precum has a nice hint of fruit to it. Also if he cums in my mouth it tastes like, um... I don't really know how to describe that exactly, because I guess maybe it's one of those things you have to experience to understand?

It has a faint sweetness, with a slight hint of saltiness, and then it's more of a consistency thing, you know? It's smooth, kind of creamy, but with a little extra thickness. I don't know if every guy's cum tastes like that, but I know what Daddy's cum tastes like. I've read on the internet that part of it is eating a clean diet, which Daddy and I do. Lots of veggies and not a lot of processed food, but no asparagus, though sometimes we eat asparagus and I like it when Daddy makes it.

And...

"No," Daddy says to me, apparently reading my mind. "I forbid you from ever talking to my sister about what a penis tastes like."

"Yes, Daddy," I say, apologizing. "Sorry, Daddy."

And... last message!

"Fifififi-Fiona! You didn't get kidnapped, did you? I thought Dave looked a little... I don't know. I can see why you were into him, but he didn't look like the rest of the people at the party. What college does he go to? I guess he goes to mine but I've never seen him around. I mean, I haven't seen everyone who goes to my college, so that doesn't mean much. I should ask Porter, huh? They're friends?"

"Please tell me you aren't kidnapped, though. I don't know what I'll tell Daddy if you got kidnapped. He'll be so mad at me. Fiona, call me back! Or text me. Or send me a cute Snapchat of you and Dave cuddling in bed. Just don't make it public on your story, alright? Daddy can see those, but I don't know if he looks at Snapchat a lot. I'll keep your secret, but if I don't hear from you soon..."

The message cuts off after that, I think because it's too long.

I switch back to texts and, yup.

"Too lazy to keep calling you."

"Here's a text."

"This is a text, too."

"Don't be kidnapped."

"Dave if you're reading this, my big brother owns, like, twelve guns, and he knows martial arts. He's an MMA fighter. We have ties to the mafia and the FBI and the Yakuza. That's the Japanese one. And the bratwurst."

"Auto-correct. Bratva! The Russian dudes?"

Daddy snorts and shakes his head. "Wow, I'm impressive, huh?"

"Of course you are!" I say, grinning at him. "Just, um... maybe not with twelve guns and ties to every criminal and government agency in the world."

"Not every one," he says. "She didn't add the NSA, CIA, Mexican Cartels, a bunch of motorcycle gangs..."

"What about the bratwurst, though?" I ask, super serious.

"You want my bratwurst? Yeah... keep it up, Fiona."

Daddy nudges me with his still hard cock, pressing tight against my hip. I do kind of want Daddy's *bratwurst* right now, but... I should probably text Emily back.

I poke his shoulder and try to wriggle away, but he grabs my hip and holds me tight, cuddling close.

I text my best friend fast. Just the basics, because, um... I don't know what else to say?

"I'm alive. I'm not kidnapped. Everything's good!"

Which I think should be the end of that, but then she calls me immediately and in my confused, sort of awake, happy to be cozy and cuddling with Daddy state, I... I answer the phone.

"Fiona!" Emily says, basically shouting so loud that I don't know if I even need my phone to hear her. "Oh my gosh, where are you? Are you still with Dave? What do you want me to tell Daddy? You should come here first and then we'll go meet up with him together."

Also I accidentally hit the speakerphone button. Daddy accidentally laughs at Emily being a goofball, which wouldn't usually be an issue, except... Dave and all, so...

"Wait," Emily says, stumbling on her words. "That... that was Daddy's laugh... Daddy, nothing happened. Fiona didn't stay overnight with a boy. Actually I think Dave is a girl, right? Fiona?"

"Yeah, nice try," Daddy says, shaking his head even though Emily can't see him.

"Um, I came back to the hotel last night?" I offer. That sounds reasonable, right? "I walked with Dave for a little and we talked and then he got me an Uber back to Daddy's hotel and... ta da! I'm here. Hurray!"

Daddy rolls his eyes at me. Well, you know what, Daddy? I think it's a hurray moment. And we did come back to the hotel. We didn't take an Uber, so that's kind of lying. I really don't like lying. I'm sorry, Emily! This is all confusing and awful and...

"Cool, um..." Emily says, thinking. "So are we getting

breakfast? I'll come to the hotel. We can talk about Dave. Not that we need to talk about Dave privately without Daddy around or anything. Nope. That's--"

"And Porter," I add, completely giving her away. "You're definitely going to have to tell Daddy about him."

"Fiona!" Emily shrieks. "Ugh! I... I didn't do anything, Daddy! Porter is really nice. We just talked. No kissing or anything. Just talking. We talked about really sweet things like... like farm animals and flowers, but not roses or anything. Really sweet and innocent and not even romantic flowers. Not romantic farm animals, either."

"You spent all night talking to a boy about cows and dandelions or something?" Daddy asks her.

"Sure...?" she says, nervous.

"And she kissed him," I add, because I'm a brat.

Also she did it first! I mean, I know Daddy already knows about "Dave" but... technically he already knows about Porter, too. So it's not like I'm giving anything away. Emily doesn't know that, though.

"Fiona!" Emily shouts. "I did not!"

"Did too."

"Did not!"

"Yup!"

"Nope!"

"Can you two stop yelling and hang up with each other so we can all get showered up, dressed, and go eat breakfast," Daddy says, being the voice of reason.

"Yes, Daddy," I say. "Sorry."

"Alright," Emily says, pouty. "Sorry, Daddy. I'll be quick. Maybe not too quick since it's two of you and it's not like you'll be showering together, so I've got time, and... wait, you aren't showering together, right?"

Daddy gives me a look. I also give him a look. Are we showering together? Um... yes. Yes please? Yes. Pretty please?

"No," we both say at the same time.

"Emily, that's weird," I add.

"Well, I don't know!" she says, with a shrug in her voice. "You could wear bathing suits or something. Maybe the shower's huge?"

"Yeah, still weird," Daddy says. "Also probably wildly inappropriate, so..."

"Yeah, Dave might not like that," Emily says, trying to laugh it off. "It's not like, um... I mean, no, that's weird, huh? But you and Fiona get along well so I don't know. It's not that weird, maybe? No, probably still weird. Sorry. I don't know what I'm... alright, going to go now! Bye!"

And then she hangs up. Daddy and I stare at each other, back and forth. Did that just happen? Yes, yes it did.

"Was that a test maybe?" I ask him. "Like... did Emily want to see our reactions or..."

Daddy shrugs and pulls me tight against him, spooning with me.

"I don't know," he says. "I think she's probably nervous about 'Dave' and what I'll think. She probably said just a little too much, or at least more than she wanted to. Knowing Emily it made more sense in her head before she said it out loud, and when she started talking she realized what she was saying and tried to fix it, but just dug herself in deeper."

I nod a little and relax in Daddy's warm, cuddly embrace. I think that's probably true, because Emily is like that a lot of the time, but...

I just wonder if she would be alright with me dating Daddy? I mean, it kind of sounded like it, right? Except she didn't mention dating. Or sex. No kissing, either. Just showering. Kind of. With bathing suits? Except who showers in a bathing suit? So is it fine if Daddy and I shower together? I mean, obviously it's fine because... Daddy and I shower together all the time. Most of the time, even. Except when I'm sleepy and Daddy has to go to work and then he showers on his own, but I try not to be sleepy and I try to wake up so I can shower with him before he leaves for the day, and...

I'm maybe reading too much into all of this. I don't know what Emily thinks, but I don't want her to be angry at me when she finds out that Daddy and I are dating.

I hope she's not. I hope she's happy.

We're going to tell her soon and we'll find out then.

...Right?

GREY

F iona and I shower together, obviously. This is basically the highlight of most of my mornings. I don't hate my job or anything. I mean, it's fun being your own boss, owning your own company, all of that. Stressful sometimes, especially when you have deadlines or a bunch of bullshit pops up, but it's still good.

It's mine, and I own it, and that's something I'm proud of. I didn't create it, my parents did, but I built the company into what it is now. I think they'd be proud of me. I wish they could see what I'm doing and where I'm at. Maybe they can somehow. I don't know.

This isn't about that, though. This is about the fact that showering in the morning with Fiona is pretty fucking amazing. No fucking going on, though. We've got shit to do. This is strictly business at the moment, or as business-like as we can both be when we're completely naked, bodies glistening from the shower, both of us wrapped up in steam in more ways than one.

Seriously, how the fuck did I get to be this lucky? No clue. I'll take it, though.

My favorite part about showering with Fiona is how she always wants to make sure everything is perfect. I don't even fucking know how she does it. She's magic, that's how. I'd be willing to bet that's it.

She twists the knob to start the shower, and after a few adjustments here and there, testing the water as she goes, she gets it to the perfect temperature. I stand outside, waiting and watching, letting her do her thing. Once she's done, she slips out, does this little tiptoe hop about she likes to do, just a quick up and down, lifting her heels and standing on the balls of her feet, and then she smiles up at me.

"It's perfect," she declares, and I already know it is without checking for myself.

We strip down, but Fiona likes it when we take off each other's clothes. Who am I to argue with that? Yeah, never going to do it. Also our clothes consist of bathrobes right now, so it's not exactly hard. She unties my fluffy belt and then hurries behind me to pull my robe off. After she hangs it up on a hook on the back of the bathroom door, I do the same for her.

I'm a little more insistent, though. I wrap my fingers around her tied off belt and tug her close to me. Kissing her without warning, I wait for her to gasp, mouth dropping open, before I untie her bathrobe. When she starts to kiss me back, I pull away. Hands on her shoulders, I peel the bathrobe down her arms and then let it fall to the ground.

We stand there, both of us naked. I do my best not to give her any ideas, but, uh... yeah, I'm sporting a monstrous hard-on right now. Just fucking bobbing there, pointing directly at her belly button. Fiona stares at me with lust and a little bit of awe in her eyes. When my cock throbs and bounces slightly, tapping against her stomach, she lowers her stare. Now there's lust *and* a lot of awe in her eyes.

She looks like she's ready to just get on her knees and take my cock in her mouth without a second's hesitation, but I reach under one of her arms and pull her back up.

"Not right now," I say, grinning. "Later, baby."

"Alright, Daddy," she says, my perfect little good girl. "I can be quick, though. If you want..."

Yeah. I want. I want that so fucking bad it hurts, but I also don't want to make my sister wait, especially since she's coming to the hotel to meet us. Since Fiona and I are already here, we should sort of be done a lot quicker and be downstairs by the time Emily shows up, so...

I shake my head and my cock does a teasing shake along with me. Yeah, that's really not helping. Way to fucking go, cock. Fuck off.

Fiona giggles as both heads shake back and forth, top and bottom. She's a good girl for me, though. Pulling the shower curtain back, she hops in quick. I step in behind her and away we go.

It's a shower. There's not much more to it. Seriously, I just fucking said that Fiona and I weren't going to screw around right now. I'm not lying. Believe me, I wish I were lying. I'm not, though. This is a shower.

Showering with her is still amazing, though. She soaps me up from head to toe, scrubbing every inch of my tired body with a small handcloth. And yeah, I'm tired because we just woke up, and also tired because of what we did last night. Which... so part of that is because we stayed up late, and the other part is because we had some amazing orgasms together. Plus cuddling. Cuddling doesn't make me tired, but I felt like I should add that one in there.

While she washes me, I pour a little shampoo into my palm and then press my hands together, making some suds of my own. I run my fingers and the shampoo through her hair and she scrubs me down.

Just like that. Just the two of us. I don't know what to say here. We've got this down. Taking a shower with Fiona is one of my guilty pleasures. It's also pretty fast. Most days when we take a shower together like this it takes less time than it would if I took a shower alone. I don't know how that works. Don't ask. It just does.

So... that's not entirely true. It's true when all we do is shower. It's not true when we get caught up in the moment and I spin her around, bend her over, and fuck the shit out of her while the shower rains down on us, neither of us caring what the fuck else is happening except for the fact that we can't hold back anymore and we need each other.

There's a lot more to it. I'm a huge fan, though. I mean, I feel like Fiona's my biggest fan and I'm her biggest fan, so that's going great. Also I love her so fucking much. And... the shower stuff is a great bonus.

There's other stuff, too. Kitchen counter stuff? Fuck yeah. Living room coffee table stuff? Uh huh. On top of the washing machine as it bounces around with a full load? Mhm...

Probably shouldn't tell Emily any of this. Don't worry, I'm not planning on it.

We finish cleaning each other and rinsing off. I twist the knobs and stop the shower. Fiona gets cold really fast once the warm water isn't heating her up anymore, so I make sure to grab a towel and wrap it around her before she starts shivering. Seriously, it could be a hundred degrees out and she'd still start shivering after getting out of a hot shower.

It's fine. I'll keep her warm. She's my baby girl, after all. Mine.

I grab my own towel and dry off fast. Fiona has her towel and she's trying to dry off, but she's a lot slowerI step out of the shower and Fiona's about to step out on her own, but I put a stop to that real quick. Wrapping my towel around my waist and tying it off, I reach in and scoop her up into my arms, her towel and all. I carry her off to the bedroom, toss her onto the bed, and cover her ass with blankets.

That's a figure of speech, by the way. More than her ass is covered. She's basically covered from chin to toe in heavy blankets, and she's still fucking shivering, so...

"Warm up," I tell her, smiling softly. "I'll get your toothbrush."

"Thank you, Daddy," she says, teeth chattering.

And I do that. Teeth get brushed. She stops shivering eventually. We get dressed, Fiona does her makeup magic voodoo or whatever the fuck girls do. I don't really know the difference. She looks beautiful as fuck without makeup, and then she looks beautiful as fuck with makeup. I guess it's a different kind of beautiful as fuck, but still, both ways are beautiful as fuck and I don't really care which is which.

Fiona likes her makeup, though. She says she wants to look pretty for me. I appreciate that, but she'll always look pretty to me no matter what.

Also today she decides to wear regular clothes. Just a pair of jeans and a cute t-shirt with sneakers. The t-shirt matches her sneakers, both of which are pink. Also the t-shirt says "Cute" on it. That's it. Pink t-shirt with "Cute" in white letters.

"Really?" I ask, taking this moment to not only shake my head at her t-shirt but also to ogle her breasts.

"I'm cute," she says, matter-of-fact, pointing to the word on her shirt.

"I know you're cute," I tell her. "I've seen you naked."

"I'm cute with clothes on, too!" she adds, laughing at me.

"Well yeah, I've also seen you with clothes on."

"See?" she says, half ignoring me. "It says it right here?" She takes a moment to hold up her breasts with her hands. Or she's underlining the word. Whatever. "C-U-T-E. Cute."

"If you don't cut it out, I'm going to fuck the cute out of you," I growl at her.

"Nooooo, Daddy, I like being cute."

"How about just fuck you, then?" I offer.

Compromise is important in every relationship; remember that, it's important.

"Alright," she says with a nod. "Deal."

"Except we're going to breakfast," I add.

"I mean, we can do that or I can accidentally pull down my pants and bed over the bed and you could accidentally do the same and then trip and if your cock accidentally thrusts hard inside me and then it takes us a little while to get up because we're stuck, um..."

"You really put a lot of effort into that one, huh?" I ask, grinning.

"It could happen accidentally!" she protests, holding back a giggle.

"Yeah, alright, Little Miss Cute. We'll see how that accidentally goes later. Right now we're going to breakfast."

"Aww," she says, pouting at me.

I have no words to explain how much of a fucking turn on it is when Fiona pouts at me. Seriously, no fucking words. She does things to me, man. It's rough.

Also I don't want her to be too pouty, so as we walk to our hotel room door, I reach back and swat her ass quick. She hops up and yelps, then glares at me with a silly smirk on her face.

"Better?" I ask.

"Uh huh!" she murmurs.

The smile sticks on her face the entire way to the lobby. Yeah, picture this. We're walking down the hall to the elevator and she just can't stop smiling. Get into the elevator? Smiling all the way down. No one's in the elevator, but still she smiles.

We step out on the lobby level floor and look around for the restaurant. Fiona's still smiling, or she was, but then she turns into an angry cat or something. I glance the way she's looking and see Holly walking down the hall towards us.

Holly smiles, Fiona practically hisses, and I'm stuck between the two of them. Yeah, I don't really know what the fuck to do in a situation like this. Holly helped me out, but I also love Fiona, so...

Holly ignores Fiona for the time being, starts to wink at me, and...

Fiona clings to my arm, possessive, holding me tight. Look, I'm not even fucking going anywhere! I'm right here, so...

Holly's mind goes through a series of churning thoughts, some kind of sudden dawning flashing in her eyes. She takes one more quick look at me, then glances at Fiona, and finally takes the two of us in together.

"Ohhhhhh," she says, as if the world and everything makes perfect sense now. "She's not your daughter, is she?"

Fiona, always one with words, says, "He's mine!"

Also she's still clinging to me. Pretty sure I'm about to lose circulation in my arm soon. Oh well. Not much I can do about it now. Do I really need two arms?

"Uh, yeah..." I say, because I probably should have said this before. "Fiona's not my daughter."

In my defense, I never thought it'd become an issue. You don't exactly go around telling random strangers that someone isn't your daughter, do you? Yeah, didn't think so.

"He's my Daddy, though," Fiona adds, sassy as fuck.

Holly raises one eyebrow and tosses Fiona an appreciative grin. "Really now? Sounds kinky."

Fiona nods. "It is," she says, matter-of-fact.

Yeah, this girl, what a fucking brat. We get it, Fiona. You like being spanked. I mean, I like spanking you, so pretty sure it all works out in the end. Not exactly sure this is appropriate casual conversation for a hotel lobby, but apparently no one cares what I think.

And, you know, me being an idiot, I speak before thinking, so...

"Cut that shit out before I spank your ass again," I say.

Fiona looks up at me, pouty, bottom lip thoroughly tucked between her teeth. Fuck, man...

"Yup, definitely kinky," Holly says, split between a sigh and laughing. "I'm always too late for the good ones. Oh well."

Fiona perks up at that. She gives Holly a curious stare and Holly just shrugs, accepting defeat. Yeah, there you go. Are you happy now, Fiona? I was all yours to begin with, but now I'm all yours again. Basically nothing has changed, but suddenly she seems a million times happier with everything around her.

"Our room was really nice, though," Fiona says, a little louder than a whisper. "Thank you. I liked the whirlpool and the balcony."

"The whirlpool, huh?" Holly asks, laughing. "You two had time to use that after that crazy frat party?"

"Yup!" Fiona says, giddy. "We made lots of bubbles, too."

"Fiona!" I snap. Because, yeah, we aren't talking about the bubbles. Where did they go? How did we get rid of them? It's better if you don't know. Trust me.

"Bubbles, eh?" Holly says, a curious admiration in her voice. "I really am always too late for the good ones."

"You will find someone good," Fiona tells her. "Don't worry."

"Aw, thanks, hun."

"We were, uh... looking for the restaurant for breakfast?" I add. "Any help there?"

"I was heading in that direction, actually. Let's go. I'll see if I can get you a good table. Is your sister coming? That one's actually your sister, right?"

"Yeah," I say. "Emily's my sister. Fiona's her best friend. Uh... and Fiona and I are, you know, dating, so... that's complicated."

"Don't tell Emily please," Fiona adds. "Not yet."

"Oh, don't worry. Your secret's safe with me," Holly says. "I guess I should have realized more was going on what with the extreme measures you took to get into that party last night, Grey."

I shrug, nonchalant. No big deal. Just going to save Fiona from horny frat guys. It happens.

Or not. Seriously, *not*. Please don't fucking do this shit to me again, Fiona. Once is plenty. I'll just fucking sneak into the party straight from the start next time. I'll go as your date. I don't fucking care. I just don't want a repeat performance of last night.

Also she's working off that money I used to pay for her. Don't worry, pretty sure she's going to love every minute of it. Yeah... I've got some great ideas for later.

Fiona cleaning the house in a sexy maid outfit without panties on?

Yes. But that's just the start...

FIONA

Daddy's mine and I'm his good girl but also we're at breakfast and Emily just showed up, so...

I am very sad that I can't cling to Daddy anymore. I'll cling to him extra later, though. Sorry, Daddy. A girl has needs, and sometimes those needs involve cuddling with her Daddy. That's just the way the world works, you know?

A waiter brings over our juice. Daddy always drinks grapefruit juice in the morning, but I like orange juice. Emily asks for an orange juice when she sits down, too.

She huffs, picking up the menu, pretends to look at it for a few seconds, and then puts it back down on the table.

"Hi," she says, still very huffy.

"Yeah, hey," Daddy says, ignoring her attitude.

"Hi, Emily," I say with a smile.

"You two are being weird," she says, eyeballing both of us.

"Um... no..." I say, nervously shaking my head.

"You're the weird one," Daddy says. "What the fuck was up with the dress you stuffed Fiona in? And you had a matching one? Yeah... don't fucking do that shit."

"Don't do what stuff?" Emily asks, but I'm pretty sure this is a rhetorical question. "We're adults, Grey! We can go to parties if we want to, and... we can wear dresses like that all the time!"

"Oh yeah?" Daddy asks, staring her down.

"Um... maybe?" Emily answers, nibbling on her bottom lip.

"Look, it's not about independence or whatever you want to call it," he says, putting on his very logical big brother voice. "I worry about you two, alright? And when you go to frat parties in dresses that are made to show off your tits and your ass, uh... yeah, I worry even more. So, please, don't fucking do that shit."

"Oh," Emily says, staring down at her breakfast menu. "Sorry. Um... everything was fine, though. I think you're worrying over nothing."

"Everything went fine?" Daddy asks, but he's not actually asking a question. "How about Fiona going out with some guy named Dave? What's that about?"

And... that's not really playing fair, but maybe Daddy has a point. I mean, he does have a point. Before I went into the Seven Minutes in Heaven room, I had no idea who the guy on the other side was. Thankfully it was Daddy, but what if it was someone else?

"He seemed nice," Emily says, unsure how to proceed. "And... well, it's not like she had sex with him, Grey." She hesitates, looking to me for confirmation. I've already lied enough! I just keep my mouth shut and stare at my menu like a good girl. "Wait, you didn't have sex with him, did you?" she asks, both shocked, excited, and completely caught off guard.

I mumble something. Mumble mumble! Mumble? And then I say, "He was a perfect gentleman!"

Which is true. Daddy's always been a perfect gentleman to me. I love you, Daddy.

"Yeah?" Daddy asks, somehow keeping a straight face and not giving everything away. How does he do that? I don't know. Daddy's impressive. "A perfect gentleman? I don't know about that one..."

"What would you even know?" Emily asks, going from sulking to sassy in two seconds flat. "You weren't there. What did you do last night, by the way?"

Notice how she artfully changed the subject? Yup. Emily and I look out for each other. Usually. I'm really bad at this when it comes to Daddy, though. I basically tell him everything. I'm sorry, Emily!

"Oh, you know," Daddy says with a shrug. "Had a few drinks. Settled into a nice bubble bath. Put on my bathrobe and went out onto the balcony to look up at the stars for awhile. Nice night."

"Wow," Emily says with the most indifferent, bored voice possible. "Yawn. Lame. Wait, where'd you get a bathrobe? You guys have a balcony in your room? What the heck?"

"We do!" I say, excited. "We got a room upgrade or something, right, Daddy?"

He nods like this happens all the time. Aw yeah.

"That's cool," Emily says. "The rest is pretty lame, but the upgrade is cool."

I shrug. "I don't know. I like bubble baths and stargazing and bathrobes. I think it sounds like a nice night."

"Thank you, Fiona," Daddy says, smiling at me.

"You're welcome, Daddy," I say.

"Ugh. Gag. Get a room, you two," Emily says. "Oh, wait! Ha!"

"That's not funny, Emily!" I say, pointing at her. A really hard point, too! Grrr!

"What are you getting for breakfast, by the way?"

"Um... I was looking at the stuffed French toast."

"Ooh, that looks good. What about you, Daddy?" she asks him.

"Eggs benedict with corned beef hash," he says.

"Ugh. You've both picked already. Alright, um... let me see..."

When the waiter comes back, we each order our food. We enjoy our breakfast together. I sit next to Daddy and Emily sits next to me. It's really nice. It's like we're a family, but in a different way, and...

I hope it will always be like this. I really like it.

I had a lot of fun last night, but I think me and Daddy and Emily could have fun like we used to, too. Together, just hanging out, doing whatever fun stuff that we want to do.

She won't be mad that I'm dating Daddy, right?

A NOTE FROM MIA

Make sure you don't miss any of my new releases by
signing up for my VIP readers list!
Cherrylily.com/Mia

You can also find me on Facebook for more sneak peeks
and updates here:
Facebook.com/MiaClarkWrites

We made it to the end!

If this is your first time reading one of my books, um…
woo boy! You're in for a wild ride when you go to check
out the rest, haha.

I'd definitely recommend going to check out Daddy
Issues if you want to see how Grey and Fiona came
together in the first place. I wanted Daddy's Little Angel to
stand on its own, so sometimes I just made quick refer-

ences to Daddy Issues instead of going crazy. When you check out Daddy Issues you can see what all of those are about, though.

I'd also recommend my Stepbrother With Benefits series! That's a really wild and crazy ride, haha. Ethan and Ashley's story is intense and there's a ton of it, so if you're looking for something to really sink your teeth into then I know you're going to love it.

But enough about that. Let's talk more about Daddy's Little Angel.

I like holiday stories, but usually I don't like them to be too heavy handed about the holiday they're about, you know? So I don't know if this is a Valentine's Day story so much as a story that happens to have a Valentine's Day party in it, haha.

Mostly, I thought it'd be fun to screw with Grey and Fiona. That's what they get for not telling Emily they're dating. Also, do you think Emily knows? I mean, sometimes she seems a little oblivious, and then other times she says things that are maybe a little too spot on, so…

We shall see! Actually, I really do want to see, haha. I'm planning on a new story with Grey and Fiona where we figure all of that out and deal with even more craziness involving Grey and Fiona hiding their relationship.

I thought I'd help them out a little in this one, though. Obviously Grey's new friends from Emily's college know what's going on. And Holly knows by the end. Porter is getting pretty close to Emily, too… will he tell her?

Don't do it, Porter! I think Grey and Fiona have to tell Emily on their own.

They've probably got to tell a lot of people, though. I mean, there's the yoga class that Grey and Fiona go to. Plus there's Grey's business friends. I don't know if they really need to know, but that could be fun. And then there's Fiona's mother, which, um…

I won't get too into that one. Check out Daddy Issues if you want to know more of the backstory there.

Also, we'll obviously need more punishments! They'll be sexy ones, don't worry. I'm sure Grey has ideas, and I'm sure Fiona will be a brat, and I'm sure they'll explore new ways to have fun together, and…

Next time!

I'm really glad everyone's enjoyed Grey and Fiona's story, though. I wasn't sure how it would turn out when I first wrote about them, but I've gotten so much great feedback and requests for more. I'd definitely like to see what's in store for their future and write more books about them. Let me know what you think!

I want to write more characters that you fall in love with too, though. There's a place for both, I think.

If you enjoyed Grey and Fiona's story, I'd love if you could leave me a review to let me know what you think. They really help and I enjoy reading them, too. It also helps me figure out what to write more of in the future.

What did you think of Grey and Fiona's wild side? Grey's really protective of her, but I know he's also worried about what his sister will think. Do you think Emily knows? How about that whole Porter and Emily situation? Is it meant to be for them?

How should Fiona stake her claim on Grey in the

future to avoid more situations like the one with Holly? And I don't know if her and Emily should go to anymore frat parties. Or maybe they should and Grey sneaks in earlier again? Maybe "Dave" will make a future cameo? Haha.

I hope you enjoyed the story and that you're excited about Grey and Fiona! Definitely let me know what you think.

Thanks again for reading. I really appreciate it!

Bye for now!

~Mia

ABOUT THE AUTHOR

Mia likes to have fun in all aspects of her life. Whether she's out enjoying the beautiful weather or spending time at home reading a book, a smile is never far from her face. She's prone to randomly laughing at nothing in particular except for whatever idea amuses her at any given moment.

Sometimes you just need to enjoy life, right?

She loves to read, dance, and explore outdoors. Chamomile tea and bubble baths are two of her favorite things. Flowers are especially nice, and she could get lost in a garden if it's big enough and no one's around to remind her that there are other things to do.

She lives in New Hampshire, where the weather is beautiful and the autumn colors are amazing.

You can find the rest of her books at:

www.amazon.com/author/mia-clark

You can also email her any time at Mia@Cherrylily.com if you have questions, comments, or if you'd just like to say hi!

Made in the USA
Monee, IL
08 April 2022

94346771R00157